# BLOOD MOTHERS

A DS KATE HAMILTON CRIME THRILLER

GAYE MAGUIRE

**INKUBATOR**
**BOOKS**

Published by Inkubator Books
www.inkubatorbooks.com

ISBN (eBook): 978-1-83756-088-2
ISBN (Paperback): 978-1-83756-089-9
ISBN (Hardback): 978-1-83756-090-5

# PROLOGUE
## JANUARY 2010

The knife is long and narrow. In the soft lamplight of the bedroom it glints brightly through the red film that coats the blade. This is his first face-to-face kill, and it's proved to be easier than he had anticipated. *The woman was so trusting, so foolish.*

He'd shadowed her for days until his moment came.

"May I help you with that?"

She was reaching vainly up to the top shelf for a bottle of Merlot. She smiled as he handed it to her.

*Her face is still pretty, the girl in the old photograph.*

"You're very kind," she said.

"Looks like some classy wine," he said, placing the bottle in her basket.

"It *is* a nice one. I don't know why they've moved it up so high. Would you mind getting me down another one, please? There's a discount for two."

"Sure thing, sounds like a bargain."

"You should try it, I don't know a lot about wine, but it's a lovely smooth fruity one." She blushed, like she hadn't spoken to a man for some time.

"I will, thanks for the recommendation."

He had to force himself to wait before his next move, but he had plenty to keep him busy, others to find. Four days later, trailing two behind her in the checkout line, he overheard something that meant a change of plan.

"How are you, Mrs C?"

The supermarket worker seemed to know most of the customers, and she had a personal word for many of them. He found it yet another oddity about this place, the casual friendliness, and it unnerved him. *Will she remember me?* He pulled his beanie hat lower, and his wool scarf higher.

"I'm grand, thanks, Linda. I'm off to Galway for a few days; these are for my sister." The woman lifted a huge bouquet of flowers, complete with a water-filled container, onto the counter for scanning.

"Ooh, lovely, I hope you get the weather!"

"I doubt it. It always rains in the west! Bye for now."

With that she scooped up the flowers, her two bags of groceries and a purse, and headed towards the exit. He abandoned his basket of random goods and caught up with her just outside the automatic doors.

"Need some help? Looks like you've got your hands full?"

At first she looked surprised; then recognition lit up her face.

"Oh, hello again. I've done the usual thing, I thought I'd leave the car at home and get a bit of exercise, but of course you go in for one thing and come out with a dozen."

"Let me take these two bags; you don't want to drop those nice Merlots," he said.

"Oh my God, you must think I'm a terrible lush! These are not for me, I promise." Blushing, she surrendered the two laden bags.

"I tried that wine, and it's excellent. You have good taste." He smiled as they walked towards the exit of the retail park.

"Thanks so much for your help. I'll take it from here," she said.

"Is it far? I could walk with you. I need the exercise too," he said.

She hesitated for just a moment.

"My knight in shining armour once again." She smiled, setting off. He walked with her. He already knew exactly where she lived.

Their conversation flowed easily. At the house she invited him inside, just as he'd expected. She made a phone call to cancel her plans for the evening, and they passed a pleasant hour over bowls of pasta at the kitchen table. She told him about her life. He told her nothing that was real or true. Deception was his gift. They hugged briefly as he left; she wished him luck with his search for his ancestral roots.

Barely an hour later he slipped back in through the basement door to the kitchen. It had been the work of a moment while her back was turned to jam the lock so it could be opened from the outside.

Thanks to the sedative in her wine, he found her upstairs in bed, though it was barely eight p.m. What was it the Brothers always said? *"Plan the work; work the plan."*

If only they could see him now.

# 1

DUBLIN, JANUARY 2010

"Teacher's pet..."

"More than his pet; if you ask me, the DI is getting a lot more than loyal service from her!"

"Service alright!"

The two men laughed loudly at their own joke, eliciting some attention from the crowded bar.

Maybe it was the wine, or exhaustion, but Kate's patience had run out. It wasn't the first time she'd heard acidic comments about her from certain members of the team, but they weren't even trying to keep their voices low. Half the bar could hear them. She handed her glass to Rory Gardiner, who'd just been explaining the thesis he'd written on juvenile killers for his master's degree.

"Hold this for a minute, will you?" she said.

Maybe she imagined it, but it seemed like the crowd parted before her as she walked towards Lawless and Sutton.

"Let me get you guys a drink..." she said.

The two men looked a little surprised, but their leery smiles didn't waver. Kate picked up their pint glasses, which were more than half full, raised both hands as if in salute, and tipped the beer over each man's head in a movement so swift onlookers later said it was "elegant". A cheer went up from the crowd as Lawless and Sutton spluttered and swore.

"What the fuck..."

"Stop talking shit about me, or I'll do more than wet your fucking heads, I'll have you up on harassment charges and off the force so fast you'll be lucky to get a job on the door at Coppers."

Until then it had been a good night; the Murder Squad had just closed the case of a man who had beaten his partner to death while their young child slept in the next room. With meticulous work trawling through the social media accounts of the man's known friends and family, Kate and Rory had tracked the killer down months later in Scotland, caught on camera at a party. He had been extradited and tried for murder. Just today the jury had come back after less than two hours with a guilty verdict. Kate wasn't usually a fan of work get-togethers, but since the capture and arrest had been largely down to her and Rory, she had reluctantly agreed to join the celebration.

"You should come to the pub more often, Hamilton," said Rory, handing over her wine glass. "It's normally dead boring!"

Kate drained the glass in one, keeping her back turned to Lawless and Sutton. Other team members had closed ranks around her as the two men blustered and swore. One of the more seasoned officers, a burly Cork man known to all as Silent Bob, rather forcefully bundled them out of the bar.

"No more than ye deserved, ya big gobshites," he said.

The night lasted well into the small hours, with Kate getting frequent hugs and congratulatory pats on the back from the rest of the team. The general consensus was that the two men deserved just what they got. Before the haze of drink took over, Kate was sober enough to feel grateful that her boss, Detective Inspector Jim Corcoran, had not been around to see her humiliate the two officers. She didn't know if he was aware of their constant harassment; she'd never complained to him. The repeated slur that she was his favourite, or that she'd slept her way to success, had been the last straw – as a woman on a still male-dominated force like the Garda Siochana, Kate had worked twice as hard as anyone else to get to detective sergeant on the elite Murder Squad. She'd gained a First-Class Honours degree in Forensic Psychology and Criminology, studying at night while still in uniform. She'd spent two years on secondment to the FBI Behavioral Analysis Unit in Quantico, one of only a handful of Irish police officers who'd been accepted onto the prestigious course. Now, only a few months after her return from the US, she'd scored a big win. The gruelling hard work, the almost complete lack of a personal life, and the loneliness she rarely acknowledged even to herself, had all begun to pay off. She was where she wanted to be, and nothing was going to stop her, especially not two misogynistic throwbacks.

Her phone rang at 7.45 am. She'd been fast asleep, and being awake was painful. Clumps of mascara blurred her vision, jackhammers throbbed at her head, and it was meant to be her day off.

"Hamilton, are you awake?"

It was her boss, DI Jim Corcoran.

"Yes, sir."

"We've got a murder, and I think it's right up your street," said Corcoran. "This is a big one; the media are gonna be all over it. And it's your type of thing, some sort of bloody carnage, from what I hear."

"Who's the victim?" Kate asked.

"It's a woman from Killiney, the old-money part, stabbed to death in her own bed, apparently. Look, Hamilton, I want you out there straight away."

"That might be a problem, boss," she said.

"I know it's your day off," said Corcoran, "but you'll want to be in on this one from the start, I'm sure of that."

"Can you pick me up on the way? I've no car today."

"Ten minutes, then. I'll buzz when I'm outside."

Kate spent exactly two minutes in the shower, dressed so quickly she wasn't sure her shirt was properly buttoned, and, unable to find clean socks, she'd had to put her ankle boots on without them, which would make for an uncomfortable day. She gulped down two painkillers and a half pint of cold water. Her boss was as good as his word, and the door buzzed within ten minutes. Grabbing her small bag, which held precisely one Garda-issue notebook, her ID, a couple of pens, some small evidence bags and a tin of Vicks, she locked the apartment up and hurried downstairs, her hair still dripping wet.

"You look rough, Hamilton; what's going on?" asked her boss, then threw the car into gear and pulled out into the traffic.

"Thanks for coming by, sir. I had a few jars last night, had to leave the car in town," she said.

"When will you ever learn?"

"Sorry, sir," said Kate, hoping he hadn't yet heard about the night's events. The rumour mill at HQ moved at lightning speed.

"Just get your act together, Hamilton. I'm going to need you on this one. They say it's a bloody slaughterhouse out there," said Corcoran. "I hope you're not fucking hungover because I won't have you puke on my crime scene."

Their unmarked car made steady progress through the Dublin morning traffic. A tide of commuters ebbed and flowed along the pavements, or fidgeted behind steamy windscreens in the wet streets. For the most part, they were moving against the flow, and there was no need for a siren or flashing lights. While he drove, Jim Corcoran talked.

"The victim has been identified as Irene Connolly, a widow I believe, fifty-something."

"Who found her?"

"Cleaning woman. We're talking big posh house here, Hamilton, the sort that would have a cleaning woman, probably a gardener too. Apparently she let herself in at about 7.30; the call came in at 7.36. She was pretty hysterical, by all accounts."

"Who got there first?" asked Kate.

"A couple of the lads from Cabinteely, they're *supposed* to have secured the scene. If they haven't, they'll bloody well have me to answer to."

"It should be alright," she said. "Joe Healy's the desk sergeant in Cabinteely. He's sound. He'll have warned them."

"Just so long as they didn't plant their big size twelves all over the evidence," Corcoran said.

"When you said it was a bad one, how so?" Kate asked.

"I spoke to your mate, the sergeant; the word *he* used was *mutilated*," he said. The two fell silent. It was hard not to form a mental picture of what lay ahead. Even as the adrenaline surged inside her, Kate felt an accompanying sense of dread.

# 2

Within twenty minutes the two officers were at the scene, a quiet avenue about half a mile from the coast, in one of County Dublin's most exclusive suburbs. The roads were busy as nine o'clock approached and the children of the city's elite were dropped off at expensive schools. Seaview Avenue was lined with detached homes, each different, but all prime examples of old money and good taste. At the entrance gates to "Virginia", a young Garda inspected Corcoran's ID and waved them through. Once out of the car, Kate told the Garda to keep the lawn off-limits until Technical Bureau officers could look at it. It had been raining solidly for two days; the soft earth might hold some clues.

"Best get our kit on," said Corcoran, opening the boot.

They climbed into protective suits, put on thin latex gloves and paper covers over their shoes. There was a long way to go before the Gardai could rival the US in crime scene investigation, but now that most criminals were forensically aware, the Irish force was finally catching up. The house was a large double-fronted Edwardian red-brick, with bay

windows and granite steps rising to a shiny black front door.
Inside, the wide entrance hall was tiled in black and white,
with a sweeping dark staircase. In a room on the right, they
found a guard and with him a woman, seated by the empty
fireplace. The officer crossed the room to meet them.

"Garda Sean Fallon, sir, ma'am. This is Lorraine Maher,"
said Fallon, "the cleaning lady."

The woman looked about forty, hunched in a corner of
the sofa; she had barely glanced up when they had come in.

Kate crossed the room and sat down beside her. Up close,
her round face was pale and tight with fear.

"I'm Detective Sergeant Hamilton, Lorraine, and this is
Detective Inspector Corcoran."

Lorraine blinked; her pupils were wide and unfocused.

"Can you tell us what happened?"

She didn't reply, just closed her eyes against the tears that
had begun to flow. Kate took her hand in hers. Her skin
was icy.

"What has she said?" Corcoran asked the Garda.

Fallon consulted his notebook.

"She got here around 7.30. She thought the house was
empty. Mrs Connolly was supposed to be away in Galway.
She went upstairs to get started. That's when she found
the…"

He turned aside and lowered his voice.

"…*the body, sir, in the master bedroom.*"

"Get a doctor to look at her," said Corcoran, "but not in
here. The scene has to be sealed off. Put her in my car if you
need to. We're going to need a full statement as soon as
possible."

Kate squeezed the woman's hand gently.

"You go with Garda Fallon now, Lorraine; he'll look after
you."

She followed her boss out into the hall. A knot tightened

in her stomach as they tracked up the staircase. Of the four doors on the upper corridor, only one was ajar. Corcoran nudged it open. A metallic odour wafted out. As he stopped on the threshold, she tensed behind him, drew a mask from her pocket and clipped it over her face. It was doused in clove oil, a tip she'd picked up in the US.

"Jesus Christ," said Corcoran.

He put a hand to his mouth and coughed, then put on his mask. With his shoulders blocking the door, Kate could neither get by nor see into the room beyond. Kate used the slight delay to begin preparing her camera. The forensic photographer would take hundreds of shots, but her instant prints would be useful for now. A moment later, Corcoran stepped into the room, and she finally saw the murder scene. Taking in the savage sight in front of her, Kate was glad she hadn't eaten. No amount of murder scenes had quelled her sensitive stomach, and this one was particularly disturbing.

The victim had once been a beauty, with clear skin, thick fair hair and high cheekbones. Neither age nor the killer had ravaged her face. The bulk of his handiwork had been carried out below the jawline.

"Considering the number of wounds, there's not that much blood," said Corcoran.

"That would suggest he must have done all that post-mortem," said Kate.

Her camera clicked. Through the viewfinder she could assess the scene without wanting to run from the room or throw up. She scanned the wall above the headboard and the ceiling, looking for blood splatters. There were none. The victim's blood appeared to have seeped slowly from the wounds, soaking the bedding.

"Fourteen…" Corcoran leaned forward slightly to get a better view. "Fifteen…I make it fifteen wounds," he said, "at least."

"I should think he hit every major organ."

"Maybe that's what he was trying to do, obliterate her."

"No obvious signs of a struggle."

Once more the camera flash lit up the room.

"Do you think it was sexually motivated?"

"It looks that way."

The victim was wearing what appeared to be a slip or negligee. The material was so drenched in blood it was debatable what colour it might once have been. Some of the wounds were so deep and open that her internal organs were exposed. Despite the revulsion and nausea that still gripped her, Kate was taking in every detail. While Jim Corcoran made notes, she just observed. This was going to be the most important investigation of her career, she had known that instantly, a chance to make her name in Garda HQ. More than that, she felt a kind of rage. There was something sweet and peaceful about the victim's face, as if she were just sleeping under a vivid red quilt.

The gathering clamour of sirens interrupted them. Soon, they would be displaced by the scientists. Before that, they stood, taking in a last impression of Irene Connolly's punctured body. From her throat, which seemed to have been slit, to her thighs, which were spread apart, her flesh had been slashed repeatedly. Fragments of silk soaked in blood clung to the wounds, like the wrapping paper on a butcher's joint.

"I promise we'll get the bastard who left you like this," said Corcoran.

The awful scent followed them as they left the room. Swarms of Technical Bureau officers were already at work in the hallway and on the stairs. There was a chorus of hellos and good mornings as they passed.

"Always so bloody cheerful, these techies!" muttered Corcoran.

With enormous relief Kate stepped out into the morning

air, pulled off the mask and hood, and turned her face up to the cooling rain. It felt as if she'd been holding her breath for a lifetime. Blinking as the drops hit her, she knew with certainty that for a while to come, every time she closed her eyes, this crime scene would appear inside her head.

By noon, they had called at every neighbouring house, in search of witnesses and background information, with no results. Back at the murder scene, an incident room had been set up in a police van with a computer and Wi-Fi link to HQ, and, most importantly, a kettle. Garda investigations ran on oiled wheels. That meant copious amounts of tea, coffee, biscuits, and ham and cheese sandwiches, nothing fancy. As she climbed into the van, a Garda handed her a cup of tea. It cleared her head.

Corcoran was a meticulous man and always insisted on walking through a murder scene. The Technical Bureau were thorough, but he liked to get a feel of the place himself.

He headed up towards the bedrooms and sent Kate down-stairs. The kitchen was huge, occupying the whole basement. Dozens of light beech cupboards lined the walls, the appliances were gleaming steel, the worktops were solid marble, and the floor was real terracotta. The dishwasher was empty; the SOCOs had placed the contents in evidence bags. She went to find Corcoran, who had finished upstairs and was back in the sitting room.

"She cooked for two last night, boss."

"Are you sure?"

"Pretty much, two plates with the same food residue on each, two glasses, and there were two placemats on the table."

"As far as we know, she lived alone. The husband's been dead for years, no kids, just one sister in Galway. Fallon got that much from the cleaning woman before she went all cata-tonic," he said.

"I wonder who her dinner guest was."

"Could have been our man. There could be prints or DNA on the dishes."

Corcoran went outside to the mobile unit. Kate returned to the kitchen. There was a wine rack with a few bottles of supermarket wine. In every cupboard there were gadgets of all shapes and sizes. Rich woman's toys, she thought, peering at an electric bread-maker still in its box. There were at least twenty cookbooks on a rotating shelf. The most thumbed one was Delia Smith's *Cooking for One*.

The woman in the bed upstairs was beginning to come to life here in her kitchen. Kate sat down at the table, picking the chair nearest to the radio. Closing her eyes, she tried to put herself into the mind of their victim. *You were alone a lot, weren't you? With your husband gone, what did you do in this big house? What was it that kept you here? Couldn't you bear to walk away from the past?*

Leaving the kitchen, Kate moved slowly from room to room, looking for answers; the more they could learn about the victim, the better the chances of finding her killer. Irene Connolly couldn't speak, but her photos might. They were dotted over almost every wall. In the dining room there was a wedding portrait and dozens of holiday snaps from all over the world. Irene's late husband had been a handsome man, tall and gangly as a young bridegroom, with a wide-open smile and warm eyes. They made a stunning couple. Even in the most formal pictures, the body language said the same thing: that this was a good marriage. *How had such a life ended so savagely?*

## 3

Hours later the evening papers broke the story of Irene Connolly's death. It was front-page news. "SHOCK SLAYING ON MILLIONAIRE'S ROW", "WEALTHY WIDOW STABBED" screamed the billboards as the two detectives headed back to HQ. Corcoran was incensed.

"How the hell do they know she was stabbed? Some little shit of a Garda has been blabbing his guts out for the price of a pint," he growled.

Kate bought a paper from the rain-soaked boy weaving his way through the cars. The murder victim had been a well-known socialite in her younger days; it seemed the picture editor had shots on file. On a slow news day it was a bonus, a high-profile murder victim and lots of stills just waiting to be pulled out. In the intimate setting of Dublin – in social terms, more like a small town than a European capital – this passed for a celebrity murder. Irene Connolly filled the front page, glamorous and happy, smiling directly at the camera. Inside, there was a two-page spread, with stills going back many years.

Back in HQ, poring over the coverage online, Kate tried to build on her picture of the victim. Irene had attended many charity functions, mostly children's charities and cancer care. Interestingly, her name never seemed to be linked to another man, though she'd been widowed in her early fifties. *With no children, who would benefit from the death? The house alone must be worth a couple of million, enough to be a motive for murder?*

"Right, Hamilton." Jim Corcoran interrupted her thoughts. "I've called a team meeting for six o'clock – we've got ten detectives for this one. That's the best I can do. The pathologist has released the body. She'll have preliminary post-mortem results tomorrow."

"That soon? Good."

"What have you got for me?"

"Well, not much, it's too soon. After the meeting I want to meet her sister; it's Galway, isn't it?"

"Yes, the techies found an address book," said Corcoran.

"Good, I'll head down there tonight and interview her first thing. Let's hope she has some information for us. The neighbours were useless. They weren't close, saw nothing, heard nothing!"

Corcoran slumped into a chair.

"It's always the fucking same with the wealthy, not like on an estate where everyone knows your business. Rich people don't mix with the neighbours. Lots of those big houses changed hands in the boom. Now they're full of bankrupt tycoons hiding from their creditors. No such thing as chatting over the fence," he said, snapping a pencil.

"I think you're right. It kind of adds up too, to the idea I'm getting of her."

Corcoran leaned forward.

"Come on then, give; what have you got on her?"

"It's very early days, sir; this is pure speculation."

"Go on."

"Something tells me she was lonely. A bit lost without the husband. Maybe she picked up some guy, who knows? I'll know more when I meet the sister. Has she been told?"

"The local sergeant went to the house." Corcoran slid a piece of paper across the desk. "That's the name and address. She's a widow too, and there's an adult daughter. Our victim was supposed to visit yesterday, but cancelled," said Corcoran.

"I wonder why."

"Maybe she had a date or met an old friend."

"Or a new one."

"Have you had any thoughts on our killer?"

*Patience isn't Corcoran's strong suit; how can he expect a profile with so little to work on?*

"I'm deliberately not thinking about the killer until we get the results of the post-mortem. Of course, I've got first impressions, but nothing concrete."

"Come on, we're desperate, Kate. We've got sod all to go on," he said. "No signs of a break-in; nothing seems to be missing. I could do with a handle on this bastard, and you're the closest thing we've got to a profiler. You've got two years of it to call upon, which is more than the rest of us."

"Thanks for that," said Kate. "All I can say is I've never seen anything like it. Could be sexual; we'll have to see if the post-mortem finds evidence of that. The number of wounds suggests rage or frenzy. Stabbing is personal, and this was overkill. But the wounds were inflicted post-mortem. Whoever did this is angry, very angry, but was it personal? Or a random attack?"

"You tell me...do you think she let him in? The techies haven't found any signs of a forced entry. If it's not a break-in or a bungled robbery..." Corcoran paused and ran a hand through his already messy hair; he looked grim.

Kate knew what he was thinking.

"I know. If he did it for kicks, he won't stop now," she said.

"Exactly. God forbid this psycho will strike again, because we've got fuck all to go on," he said. "They're running the prints we found, but so far there's no match. I've been around this force for more than twenty years, and I can't think of a single one like this. There were those two women in Grange Gorman a few years ago, they were more or less butchered, but we got the guy who did it; the bastard went on to kill four more before we caught him. He's never getting out."

"Any word on the victim's last movements?"

"Sweet FA at this stage; we're working on the financials and phone records. Her credit cards and cash were still in her bag. We've got CCTV from the local shopping centre. Lawless is going through it now. The Tesco receipt in the bin was timed 4.36 pm, so I think we can safely assume she was still alive yesterday afternoon." Corcoran stood up and sighed heavily. "Come on, let's brief the rest of them."

The Ops Room was stuffy, a current of excitement raising the temperature among the detectives. Most were young, late twenties upwards, and most were men. One or two were seasoned investigators, eagerness tempered with wisdom; a good mix, thought Kate. As she made her way to a seat near the back, she was aware of a dark irony: only murder created this kind of atmosphere – the pack of hounds straining to go after the fox. Richie Lawless and Joe Sutton sat together. Kate made a point of looking directly at them. *I will not be ashamed.* The two men nodded at her by way of greeting, and she felt a certain satisfaction that they looked both hungover and more than a little embarrassed. *Good.*

"Good evening, everyone." Corcoran commanded instant attention. "You all know by now why we're here. Let me fill you in on the facts, brief and all as they are."

The faces were intent, all eyes fixed on the detective inspector.

"As the photos from the Technical Bureau become available, you'll see that this was a particularly brutal killing. Multiple stab wounds."

He paused for a moment to consult his notes.

"The Technical Bureau are still at the scene and will be there for at least another day. It's a huge house that'll take some time to examine. The body is now at the mortuary, and we're hoping for preliminary findings from the post-mortem tomorrow."

With more than a hint of tiredness in his movements, Corcoran perched on the edge of a desk.

"I might as well tell you this is going to be a tough one. We've got fuck all to go on. No robbery, no obvious motive, precious little physical evidence. It means we're going to have to try that bit harder."

A few officers exchanged glances that said they'd heard those words before. Corcoran saw the looks, and it seemed to annoy him.

"It's time to get up off your arses and away from those fucking screens! The local officers are doing door-to-door. You need to liaise with the sergeant in Cabinteely. If they've turned up anything that smells off, follow up on it. Speak to any contacts you have in the area. Until such time as the lab gives us something to go on, you're going to turn over every stone in Killiney, Ballybrack, Loughlinstown, the Noggin. The local lads will point you in the right direction, but *this is our case*. Track down every local with a history of violence, anyone on remand for serious assault, or recently released. I want all of them eliminated. If we don't get a decent line of enquiry in the next two days, we may as well shut up shop and go home."

The detectives broke up into huddles, and Corcoran went from group to group, spelling out instructions. Once assignments had been handed out, Kate was on her way, picking up

her car from the city car park where she'd left it the night
before. The rain stopped as she left the confines of the city.
Rolling her window down a couple of inches, the cold rush of
wind felt good. She made it to the Galway Road in twenty
minutes; then it was a steady cruise. It was hard not to picture
the crime scene again, and the drive passed easily while she
processed the information they had about the victim in her
mind – for the moment Kate knew that with little evidence
yet of the perpetrator, getting to know the victim's life in
detail was the best option.

By the time she reached Galway, it was almost 9 pm, she
was tired and still a little hungover, and deciding it was too
late to call on the victim's sister, she checked into a city centre
hotel. Unsurprisingly on a cold, wet January night, it was
quiet and almost empty, but the receptionist promised her
there was someone in the kitchen who could rustle up something tasty from the room service menu. Gratefully Kate
ordered an omelette and decided there was time for a bath
before her food arrived. Even the warm water failed to bring
peace. Images of the day raced behind her closed eyelids. It
was no use; the bath wasn't helping at all.

Stepping out, she dried herself quickly and put on
pyjamas from the travel bag that she always kept at the ready
in her car boot. She flicked the TV remote until a news
bulletin appeared. When the room-service maid arrived, Kate
was engrossed in the extensive coverage of the murder. It was
only after the girl had gone that Kate realised she'd forgotten
to order a drink. As video footage of the Killiney house alter-
nated with stills of a younger, prettier Irene Connolly on the
screen, Kate broke the seal on the minibar. It was full, enough
booze to guarantee a long, dream-free sleep. Sighing heavily,
she grabbed a bottle of mineral water and closed the fridge
door with a slam.

The omelette was good, with a small salad and a warm

bread roll. Kate cleaned the plate. It was her first proper meal in days, and it almost made her sick. She couldn't remember the last time she'd cooked for herself. The months since her return from FBI Headquarters in Virginia had passed in a blur of work, a bit too much drinking, and nights spent mostly alone. Kate couldn't get used to it. When sleep finally came, she would dream of Greg and wake in a sweat of desire. *I should be over him by now.*

There had been something else lately that came between her and a good night's sleep. Opening her bag, she pulled out a small blue envelope postmarked a month earlier. She removed the single sheet and read the opening words again:

*Dear Kate, I'm not a madwoman or a crank. I loved you from the moment I held you in my arms, a tiny helpless little baby with no one but me to love you...*

# 4

DUBLIN, JULY 1967

Rosie Jackson had her first crush at the age of fourteen. It felt very exciting, even a little dangerous. The boy was her cousin, and though they had only just met for the first time, Rosie was besotted. *Forbidden love.* It wasn't a romance or anything, but there was definitely flirting going on, and it would be huge news to tell her friends after the school holidays, and maybe a bit of practice for when she met a real, available boy. Richard (he preferred Rick) was sixteen and came from London. He was "pissed off" with his parents for making him join the family holiday in Ireland. It was his punishment for being expelled from his second public school in three years. Rosie's parents didn't warm to him, but she loved his boldness. He smoked and used bad language in front of the adults and wore way-out clothes he said came from Carnaby Street.

On the night before the English visitors were to leave, Rosie crept downstairs. Her cousin was going to teach her to smoke. By the time she joined him in the drawing room, he'd already been at her father's brandy, and she joined him. She didn't like the taste, but it was OK with loads of lemonade. It

wasn't long before her head was swimming from the combination of two cigarettes and the alcohol. They sat together on
the fireside rug and took turns on the hand-rolled cigarette.
Rosie giggled when Richard began to fondle her breasts
through the cotton of her nightdress. At first it felt nice, but
soon he was on top of her, and she could hardly breathe with
his tongue probing her mouth. Suddenly his hands became
rough. Summoning all her concentration, Rosie pushed hard
against his chest, aware that he was tearing at her nightclothes ever more frantically. Still, she didn't quite know what
he was doing.

"Stop, Rick, stop! You're smothering me."

Her voice felt faint and far away, the words slow to form.
His fist snapped her head to one side, and the shock of the
pain silenced her. Terrified of waking the family, she didn't
even cry out when the second punch landed.

"Shut up, you little bitch, you've been asking for it all
week."

He had his trousers open and pulled down now, and
Rosie covered her face against what she might see *down there*.
Richard's left hand clenched around her throat, tight enough
to panic her. His right hand prodded her groin; then he
pushed himself inside her with a massive angry thrust. As
she gasped for breath, he kept doing it over and over, and it
was agonising. As soon as his grip on her throat loosened,
Rosie's screams brought everyone in the house down the
stairs in moments. As the light snapped on overhead, Richard
rolled off his cousin, scrambling to do up his jeans, then
pushed past the shocked family gathered in the doorway,
wrenched open the hall door and ran from the house. As her
mother knelt beside a sobbing Rosie, blood began to trickle
from between her legs, over the antique Persian rug.

Two months later, after all the recriminations and anger,
and the bitter estrangement from the English side of the

family, it began to dawn on Rosie that the rape had left her with more than nightmares to contend with. Her school skirt wouldn't close at the waist; she'd missed two periods, but hardly noticed in the midst of all the upset. Running her hands over the slight roundness of her daughter's normally flat belly, her mother, Marina, realised the awful truth. Rosie was going to have her first cousin's baby.

The scandal would mean the end of the Jackson family's social standing if it ever got out. Sean and Marina were distraught; Rosie cried for two days. Sean disappeared to work and often came home late smelling of drink. Then Marina recalled a whisper at the hairdressers', a half-heard snippet about a private clinic for girls who "got into trouble". Somehow, that gossip at the salon came back to her, and Marina Jackson set about finding a solution to her daughter's pregnancy that would give the close little family at least a chance of returning to normality. All she had to go on was the name of a doctor: Magnier, and time was running out.

By September, Rosie had not returned to school. Her father couldn't bring himself to discuss the situation. Her mother could talk of little else. The best Sean Jackson could do was an occasional pat on the shoulder or a faint smile of encouragement.

"Keep your chin up, love," he'd say.

Even these fleeting contacts were awkward and embarrassed. He spent far longer than usual at his construction company.

Desperately relieved to have found him, Marina was impressed with Mr Albert Magnier, consultant obstetrician. He looked exactly like a senior consultant should: expensive suit, well groomed, greying hair, and a smile that exuded confidence. In the waiting room outside, Rosie worried that everyone must know her dreadful secret. There was only a prim receptionist, and two women talking in loud whispers.

They seemed to enjoy swapping painful details of embar-
rassing complaints and mysterious surgeries. Her mother had
hinted at the possibility of an operation, and everything the
women said made it all the more terrifying.

Finally her mother emerged from the doctor's room and
called Rosie in. For a moment she thought she might be
having the operation there and then, but the doctor just
asked her to lie up on the couch. Then he felt her tummy,
pressing and prodding rather uncomfortably.

"OK, my dear, that'll do for today."

"You say the incident occurred in July," he said to Marina.

"Yes, mid-July."

"Mrs Jackson, your daughter is at least twelve weeks
pregnant."

"But that's not possible; it's been less than twelve weeks
since the...incident."

The doctor continued writing for a moment.

"I assure you, Mrs Jackson, your daughter is at least three
months pregnant." Marina held his gaze.

"Rose love, wait outside for me, will you?" she said.

———

ROSIE WAS GLAD TO LEAVE. She knew the doctor had upset her
mother but was unsure how. Marina knew only too well what
the doctor was implying, and suddenly it became vitally
important to convince him he was wrong. Not for an instant
did she doubt that Rosie had been a virgin before the attack,
even without the evidence she'd seen with her own eyes. The
picture of her little girl lying bleeding on the hearthrug was
not one she would easily forget.

"I will not argue with you, Mrs Jackson. It is possible, of
course, that my examination was misleading. Rose is slight of
build, and that can make the enlarged uterus seem bigger."

He wasn't conceding, but Marina was too upset to argue. She called her daughter back into the consulting room. Rosie was conscious of the whispering women with the disgusting ailments watching her curiously.

"Well, Mrs Jackson, I've explained the position to you. We can take her in from about Christmas. She'll start to show around then. I calculate the due date to be around the beginning of April, end of March, although that might vary by several weeks."

Rosie was puzzled. When would she be having her operation?

"That's a long time to spend locked away."

Rosie shot her mother an alarmed look.

"You must look upon it as a retreat, a chance for the child to get over her ordeal. And of course you may visit; we pride ourselves on the discretion of our staff."

Rosie felt rather than saw her mother give in, then it was over, and they went home by taxi, each silently worrying about the future. She wasn't sure, but it seemed like the visit to Dr Magnier, which was supposed to end the crisis, had somehow made things worse.

# 5

DUBLIN, JANUARY 2010

When the school had recommended a life in service to his mother, after young Billy Butler had failed his Primary School Certificate for the third time, she despaired. She had so hoped to make a priest or a Christian Brother of her only son, but he had been deemed a "slow learner", who simply did not measure up to the standards a seminary would require, by his teachers. So it was that Billy Butler ended up, an illiterate fourteen-year-old, at St Mary's Convent of the Daughters of the Cross in leafy Dublin 4. He came highly recommended, as the longest-serving altar boy in his parish, with glowing testimonials on his manners, piety and cleanliness.

Fifty years on, Billy was all that remained of the once-busy convent. It was more than twelve months since the last few nuns had retired to the mother house in France. Billy acted as caretaker, partly to safeguard the valuable property, but also because he had nowhere else to go, with both his parents long dead. He filled his time easily enough. He kept the votive lights shining at each statue and shrine. At night he toured the house, snuffing out the candles. As the dust accumulated on the dark wood panelling and what remained of the Victorian furniture, the old man billowed by in his hand-me-down cassock. He liked the sound of the fabric swishing around his legs, and there was no one now to scold him for aping his betters.

The modest wage he received from the order was more than enough to meet his needs. In the basement kitchen, which had always been his haunt, he could manage a fry-up or a ham sandwich. As long as there was enough money for a couple of pints in the evening, he was content. And now that he had a fine new friend, Billy couldn't wait to get to the pub. This friend wouldn't let him put his hand in his pocket to buy a drink. No one had ever taken such an interest in Billy. The old man had years of silence to make up for, years of secrets to tell.

He had rarely been so happy. Surrounded by women his whole life, he'd never been at ease with other men. It was the beer that brought him to the pub each night. Now, seated in the snug with the American, there was never a moment when he envied the other drinkers. His new friend was interested in everything Billy had to say, no matter how inconsequential.

On the third night of their acquaintance, thanks to the visitor's largesse, the old man drank five pints of stout. It was more than double his usual intake, and by closing time he was falling asleep.

"What'll we do with you, Billy?" said the barman, who'd known Billy for many years, as he tried to get him to his feet.

The American stood up, put Billy's arm over his shoulders, and began to walk him towards the door.

"Can you manage him on your own?" asked the barman.

"No problem," said the American. "I'll see that he gets home.".

"Grand so, it's only a few minutes away, take a left around the corner, then keep going all the way to the end of the avenue. St Mary's is the last on the right with the big gates. You can't miss it."

As the night air hit him, Billy shook himself and set off unsteadily, his minder's arm linked in his. The old convent building loomed through the trees behind a high wall. Billy fumbled a huge key from the pocket of his cassock. Ignoring the gates, he led the way to a wooden door set into the high wall a few yards away. Inside, the lawn glistened, the rain having given way to a clear bright moon. Long, wet grasses brushed the men's legs as they made their way along stepping stones through the overgrown garden. Twice the American stumbled. The old man seemed to know every bump and hollow. Eventually, after circling the building, they came to a flight of steps leading to the basement. As Billy's key turned in the lock, he was puzzled to find the other man still with him.

"I'll just see you in, make sure you're OK," said the American.

It was a moment's work to settle the old man in his cell-like room off the kitchen. Once he caught sight of it, Billy more or less collapsed onto the narrow bed. The American prised off the worn black leather shoes and left Billy snoring loudly, his mouth open. A sense of calm descended on the American as he explored. To him the air bristled with the soft whispers of countless women, young and old. On an upper floor he found what seemed to be an infirmary, with curtained beds and a sluice room. The voices became a cacophony. He had to lie down. The rubber-covered mattress was dusty and made him cough, and there was no pillow. He curled on his side and closed his eyes, but it didn't shut out the voices. Breathing in the scents and sounds of an imagined past, he felt again the familiar taste of rage.

# 6

It was late afternoon before Kate squeezed her car into the single available space at Garda HQ in Harcourt Street. Uninterested in food and anxious to get back to Dublin, she hadn't bothered to break the journey. En route, she replayed the interview with the victim's family on her voice recorder. After listening right through twice, she had to admit to herself that there was little to show for her long trip to Galway. The victim's sister and her niece, whom Kate had interviewed at length, had given precious little information about Irene Connolly's day-to-day life, nothing that the newspapers hadn't already revealed. Although the two women may have had the oldest motive in the book for wanting her dead, a sizeable inheritance, there was nothing to suggest they could be responsible for the killing. Not only that, they both had alibis for the day before that Kate had been able to confirm. When the murder victim had unexpectedly cancelled her visit, they'd invited two neighbours in to help eat the extra food they had prepared; the impromptu dinner party had gone on until after midnight. Kate's experience also told her that the method of killing was simply not one used by women, least of all women who seemed as normal and grief-stricken as Marion and Freda O'Sullivan.

The Ops Room was empty. Crime scene pictures covered one whole pinboard. For a second, panic struck. *Has the case been solved while I wasted my time in Galway?* Ashamed of the thought, and unable to look at the grisly montage any longer, she went in search of Jim Corcoran. She found him brooding in semi-darkness in his office.

"Well, what did you get?"

There was no disguising his disappointment when she recounted the results of her trip.

"Bloody hell, everyone has a skeleton in their cupboard," he said. "You don't just wake up one morning and get ripped to shreds in your bed by leading a quiet life."

They both knew the statistics. Most victims are murdered by someone known to them, often a close relative or spouse. Random killings by strangers are rare and usually take place in the streets or when a robbery turns nasty, and neither was the case with Irene Connolly.

"What's been going on up here?" she asked.

"Sweet feck all, that's what. That bloody shower couldn't catch a cold," he snapped, indicating the Ops Room. "Come on, I've been waiting for you. The PM is over; Harriet's ready for us."

Jim grabbed his coat, shrugged it on and was halfway down the darkened corridor by the time Kate caught up with him.

"That was quick," she said.

"She doesn't hang about. Mind you, I've been hassling her office all afternoon."

On the way to the mortuary, Kate's stomach cramped. Autopsies came with the territory, and she'd seen a good number, but that didn't mean it was easy. At least by this hour most of the procedure would be over, or so she hoped, conscious that she'd forgotten to eat all day and wouldn't be able to face food afterwards. The grey windowless block in a shabby industrial estate on the north side of Dublin gave little clue to its grisly purpose. They signed in with the porter. He knew them both by sight, but the formalities were still to be observed.

Harriet Stilson, the state pathologist, was renowned for the speed and efficiency of her work. By the time they'd put on scrubs and entered the brightly lit theatre, they were not surprised to find her writing up her notes at a desk in the corner. Meanwhile the subject of all their attention lay covered to the neck by a green sheet. Again, Kate was struck by the peaceful demeanour of the dead woman's face.

"Evening, Harriet, I see you've been busy," said Jim Corcoran.

He gestured towards the numerous phials and containers of tissue samples lined up along the pathologist's desk, neatly labelled and numbered. The doctor waved them over to sit on a bench by the wall.

"I'll be one sec, just finishing these notes...make yourselves at home."

It was impossible to keep from looking at the corpse, but they both tried. Jim took out a cigar and clamped it unlit between his lips. Kate rummaged in her bag for the Vicks and held it to her nose – the smell of death and disinfectant never failed to unnerve her. She smeared some under her nose and silently passed the little tin to Jim. Inevitably, they let their gaze come to rest on Irene Connolly's remains.

"Right – shall we do the conducted tour?" said the doctor.

They stood and followed her to the table.

"Do you want chapter and verse or edited highlights?"

It was an accepted fact among police officers that forensic pathologists fell into two camps – the miserable ones, brought down by their daily dose of death, and the cheerful ones, who manage to retain an unnerving good humour in the face of carnage. Harriet Stilson was something of a wit, and as always, Kate found her bonhomie unsettling. Not so Corcoran, who seemed to have cheered up at the prospect of some new leads.

"You can just cut to the chase, Harriet. I'm late for my dinner," he said.

"Sixteen stab wounds, all post-mortem. She actually died of asphyxiation."

"Strangled?"

"No, smothered – probably with her own pillow."

"It doesn't look like she put up a fight," said Jim.

"My guess is she was sedated or intoxicated. I can't be sure until the toxicology reports are back, but you're right – she wasn't involved in a struggle," said Harriet.

"Nothing under the fingernails?"

Harriet gestured towards the victim's pale forearms.

"I've taken scrapings, but I'm not hopeful. Take a look, not a single self-defence wound on her. I'd say, to all intents and purposes, she died peacefully in her sleep, helped on by having her oxygen supply cut off. There's no evidence of strangulation; the hyoid bone is intact, no ligature marks. All the stab wounds were inflicted post-mortem."

Harriet pulled back the sheet. Kate winced at the numerous lacerations on the torso – now all the more graphic since the excess blood had been cleaned away. Kate finally found her voice.

"Anything else of note?" she asked.

"No, not really. She was a fit, healthy woman – not a smoker, no signs of alcohol or substance abuse, should have had a good twenty or thirty more years in her."

The doctor drew up the sheet.

"So when do you think we'll have the tox results, Harriet?"

"Not quick enough for you, Jim!"

"You've been remarkably quick already, Harriet, and I do appreciate that. But we're desperate for a lead."

"We'll have some tests back in the morning. As you well know, some of them will take days or even weeks."

Kate sensed the doctor had something else to say.

"Would you hazard a guess as to what they might find?" she asked.

"Rohypnol – our old favourite. But don't quote me."

"So she could have been partially conscious but unable to defend herself," said Kate.

"If that's what he used, yes, exactly."

"Were there any signs of rape?" asked Jim.

"No contusions or bruising, I've taken swabs, but there was no sign of biological deposits, no evidence of any form of sexual assault," said Harriet, turning back to her desk.

"So no chance of a DNA profile, then?"

"Very unlikely."

Corcoran was obviously disappointed.

"Not unless your technical people have found anything at the scene. Some of my swabs might give us touch DNA, but I'd hazard a guess the body's clean."

Harriet Stilson sat at her desk. The two detectives said their goodbyes and left, dropping the surgical robes into a laundry trolley in the corridor outside.

"Shit – we're none the wiser," said Corcoran.

They passed the drive back to HQ in silence. Jim dropped her to her car, and they said goodnight, each wrapped in their own thoughts.

Kate couldn't shake a growing sense that there was a darkening cloud over Dublin that had nothing to do with the weather.

# 7

## JANUARY 2010

The morning after the big drinking session, Billy Butler woke to his first real hangover. His bones ached, his head hurt, and he couldn't face food. Startled to find his friend had stayed the night, his pale face whitened even more when the American explained why.

"Billy, I don't want to scare you, but to tell you the truth, I was a bit worried about you."

The old man sat down, his eyes wide and watery.

"Sure why would you be worried?"

"There were a few rough-looking guys hanging around outside the bar last night. You never know what these punks might do..."

Billy looked around nervously.

"I'm pretty sure those guys followed us some of the way. I came inside with you just to keep an eye on things."

The old man, visibly shaken, began fussing around the kitchen, making tea and toast. As they sat down to eat, Billy began to form an idea. He had to make the American stay another night, those gurriers might come back, and he'd be no match for them on his own. His new friend was younger and stronger. Panic gave him courage.

"I was thinking..." said Billy.

The American nodded encouragingly.

"That hotel you're staying in must cost a lot of money..."

"You're not kidding, Billy; it costs a hell of a lot. I'll have to start looking for somewhere cheaper."

"Sure why would you be doing that when you can stay here?" said Billy. There, the words were out, and he was glad of it.

"But I can't take advantage of your kindness."

"Sure isn't there more than enough room here for the two of us."

"Well, I am running a little low on funds, and I do enjoy your company, Billy; you've become a good friend."

The old man beamed with pleasure.

"We'll fix up one of the sister's rooms for you; they're the best ones."

The American left to collect his luggage, after seeing that the door was secure and checking the garden for intruders, while the old man watched from the kitchen window. Billy found a spare key to the front door for him. The house felt quiet now he was alone, and it made him nervous. Billy wondered how he'd managed on his own since the nuns had gone.

When his friend returned, he led him to a room at the front of the convent that had been the Mother Superior's. Billy had been busy, and while nothing could disguise the smell of crumbling old books and dead flowers, he had dusted and vacuumed. The bed was made up with clean white linen and an old-fashioned red satin eiderdown. Billy prattled on, pointing out the great view from this side of the house.

AS THEY STOOD in the bay window, one bent and clumsy, the other tall and still, the American looked out across the city rooftops and wondered where his search would take him next.

# 8

It was almost nine before Kate reached home. She was exhausted, and despite the sights and smells of the mortuary, which were impossible to shake, she knew she had to eat. Inside the apartment there was a light shining under the living room door. *Did I leave it on?* The room was quiet, a couple of table lamps casting a soft glow. On the couch, lying on his stomach, head buried in a cushion, was a man. Kate turned to run and banged into the coffee table in her haste, waking the man. He stood up and stumbled towards her, arms outstretched, the lamps behind him making him seem gigantic.

She was out of the room, through the front door and down the corridor in a second; then she took the stairs, almost leaping from one floor to the next. Her pursuer, after a slow start, was almost as fast. He caught up with her as she fumbled with the security doors in the entryway to the apartment complex.

"Kate! It's me!"

He'd been shouting her name down three flights of stairs, but it was only when she got to the exit that she actually heard something more than a scary roar. Then he was upon her, wrapping his arms around her. She stopped struggling. Eventually, she was able to talk.

"Jesus Christ, Greg! You scared the shit out of me!"

"I'm sorry, honey, I wanted to give you a surprise, not a heart attack!"

"How...what..." She gasped for breath. "What on earth are you doing here?"

"Shall we go back upstairs to continue the interrogation?" Greg smiled.

"No! Fuck no! Tell me right now how you got into my apartment, or I'll fucking arrest you."

He looked embarrassed.

"Your cleaning woman, Natalya?"

She nodded.

"I flashed my press card, said I was from Immigration Services, and she just rolled over and played dead."

"Christ almighty, I'll have to speak to her, stupid cow."

They took the lift back to the third floor, the small space making her feel awkward. Her mind was racing as much as her heart, and she felt absurdly giggly.

"Sorry, Kate, it wasn't funny," Greg said, flopping onto the couch.

"No, it wasn't," she said, spoiling the words with a laugh she couldn't keep in.

"Right, before you tell me why you are here, tell me you're hungry, because I am," she said.

"Always, I never refuse a good meal." He grinned.

"I didn't say anything about a *good* meal. Since you've already made yourself at home, have you *seen* my fridge?"

Kate couldn't help smiling as she picked up the phone.

"Best I can do is order a couple of pizzas."

For the first time in weeks she was energised: hungry, excited, and positive, all at once. She'd almost forgotten what it felt like to be with Greg, and for the moment she was prepared to savour the feelings without going too deep. They opened a bottle of wine and talked. First, she told him about her work since her return from the US, and soon she found herself recounting the events of two nights earlier, and her issues with Lawless and Sutton. He hugged her hard. He was what her mother would have called a touchy-feely person, and now she realised she needed that affection and comfort. The only physical contact she'd had in the last six months had been a drink-fuelled one-night stand, which she instantly regretted, and the kiss on her mother's cheek in the nursing home, a gesture that might have come from anyone, for all the recognition it brought in her mother's face.

"Those bastards need paying back. Give me five minutes alone with each of them, and they'll wish they were never born," said Greg.

Kate laughed aloud at the prospect. The thought was delicious.

"Love the caveman act, Greg, but I can hardly collude in a criminal assault, you dope!" she said.

"OK then, can't you get the guys fired?"

"Maybe I could, but it wouldn't make me feel any better. They're dickheads, both of them, when it comes to women, but they're experienced officers, and the force tends to close ranks. I might end up in bigger shit than them."

"You're way too soft, Kate – this job is gonna break you."

He was serious suddenly, but so was she.

"I'm tougher than you think, Greg. You know how much this job means to me. I'm not going to let two misogynistic dinosaurs stand in my way."

The buzz of the entryphone broke the moment. It was their delivery. As they filled up on pizza and a second bottle of red wine, the mood lightened. Kate asked about his unexpected arrival. Typically, his answer was casual, as if the senior crime reporter on the *Washington Post* could drop everything and leave the US any time he wished.

"I've taken a couple of weeks between assignments. I might start on my version of the Great American Novel! At least that's what I told my editor."

"You never told me you wanted to write a book!"

"Show me a hack reporter who doesn't think they're a budding Hemmingway!"

"But why here, why Dublin?"

"I'll give you three guesses..."

"Come on, stop playing games and tell me what you're really doing here?"

The wine was making her bold.

"That's a little complicated."

Kate felt nervous, not sure if this was the direction she wanted the conversation to take.

"Hey, you know what, I don't care what brought you here," she said, standing up. "I'm just really happy to see you."

She began to clear away the pizza boxes and empty wine bottles. Greg, taking her cue, made for the drinks cabinet and got out a bottle of whiskey. Kate realised a few glasses of wine were more than enough; she didn't even feel like another drink. *Maybe I don't have a drink problem. Just a whole set of problems that make me drink.*

"Not for me, Greg, I'm stuffed."

He poured himself a small measure. Back on the couch they automatically sat close, their shoulders touching. It was like they hadn't spent the last six months apart.

"Where are your bags?" she asked.

"The airport bus took me to a hotel. Somewhere out in the suburbs, Mount something."

"Oh..."

It was hard to keep the disappointment out of her voice.

"I wasn't sure if you'd..." He seemed lost for words. "If you'd want me to stay over."

This was tricky ground. The last couple of hours had been great, but their relationship had always been "no strings". It felt like this moment might be a turning point, and that made Kate nervous.

"Of course you're welcome to stay, but if you're happier at the hotel, that's fine too," she said.

She managed to keep her voice light but warm, a small triumph considering her heart was pounding in her ears.

"You might get fed up of me, under your feet," said Greg.

"I'm not here much, and I won't be until this case is solved," said Kate. "You can have the spare room for as long as you need. I'll soon let you know if you're in the way."

"I was hoping, you see, I kinda thought we might..." he said.

For a moment she enjoyed watching him squirm; then she took his hand.

"It's not a four-star hotel, but let me show you to your room," she said, leading him towards her own bedroom.

When morning came, Kate woke in his arms. It was seven o'clock, and she had to prise herself loose from his exploring hands. While he lounged around in boxers, she rushed to dress for work, determinedly putting the prospect of more lovemaking to the back of her mind.

"What are you going to do today?" she asked over the sound of the hairdryer.

"I'll probably go by the hotel to get my things, and then do some sightseeing. How about you?"

"I'll be in the thick of things with that killing I told you about. There are so few damn leads, we'll be chasing our tails all day."

Kate checked her make-up-free face in the mirror. She was amazed to see the hint of a glow where there had only been shadows a day before. She blew Greg a kiss and headed for the door.

"Is that all I get? When I came all this way to see my best girl?"

"I'm certainly not going anywhere near that sofa while you're on it." She grinned and left before her instincts got the better of her.

## 9

E dging her car through the city streets, Kate replayed the night in her mind. She was smiling as she made her way to the Murder Squad office, but not for long. The team was gathering in the Ops Room as Jim Corcoran called for quiet. Kate quickly joined the others. Her boss was pale, his jaw was clenched, and he watched impatiently as everyone in the room turned towards him.

"There's been another murder, in Kildare."

"What sort of murder?" asked someone.

"Female victim, in her home. I'm not calling it yet, but I don't believe in coincidences, not when it comes to murder. We might be looking at our killer's second victim."

The room filled with murmurs of surprise. As a dedicated homicide team, they were acclimatised to killings, but Ireland was a relatively safe country, with low numbers of violent deaths. For the most part those killings occurred within the criminal fraternity, revenge or feud murders, shootings mostly. This kind of murder, two women in as many days, was completely out of the ordinary.

"Hamilton, you're with me; we'll attend the scene. The

rest of you keep on the Killiney murder; it's been over twenty-four hours; I need to see some results. I'll let you know if we need more support in Kildare; for the moment we'll make use of the local team."

Kate fell into step beside her boss, all thoughts of her personal life gone, her mind already forming a list of questions, and that familiar sick feeling rising in her stomach at the thought of yet another murder scene.

"Two days, two fucking days. He didn't waste much time, did he? Bastard!"

Jim Corcoran drove like a madman, using the siren and lights whenever they hit traffic. It was forty miles to the scene of the second murder, and it took less than forty minutes to get there. He'd already decided this killing was connected to the Irene Connolly case. Kate needed convincing.

"We don't know it's our man. It could be completely unrelated," she said.

"I know, but I have a feeling about this one. There are just too many coincidences. She's about the same age, and she was at home on her own. According to the local lads, she's been hacked up badly. It could be a pattern."

Jim swung the Audi out to overtake a goods lorry, accelerated past, and dipped back into the line of cars too close to the oncoming traffic for comfort. Kate closed her eyes and held her breath; she would never get used to Corcoran's driving.

"What do we know about her? The victim..."

"Deirdre something...McMahon. Probably in her fifties, I think; she's got a couple of grown-up sons living away from home. Husband is the local headmaster."

"Where was he last night?"

"On a golfing break in Wexford."

"Does he know?"

"They woke him up with the news; he's on his way back, poor bugger. Imagine that for a wake-up call!"

"Did she work, our victim?"

"Music teacher. She gave piano lessons to half the local kids. One of her pupils found her."

"How? How did they get in?"

"That was the first question I asked. Would you believe the back door wasn't locked? Par for the course, by all accounts. The Celbridge sergeant told me people still do that around here, leave their doors unlocked."

Kate thought for a moment.

"During the day maybe, but at night? You'd think she'd lock it with her husband away, wouldn't you?" she said.

"Exactly. She'd have locked the door before going to bed in an empty house. The husband's been gone since Saturday last," said Jim.

"If the door wasn't locked, then it's likely she hadn't settled down for the night. She would have locked up last thing. She was probably killed yesterday or last night."

"And she let her killer in...that's my guess, anyway. Harriet's on her way, she'll give us an estimated time of death, but I'd lay money that that woman is as cold as ice by now. Been dead ten or twelve hours at least."

Corcoran swung the wheel, bringing the car from the fast lane into the exit lane from the motorway, eliciting a chorus of protest from other vehicles.

"It fits the pattern," said Kate. "He kills them late evening or night-time. The body's not discovered 'til next morning, at the earliest, by which time he's long gone."

"See what I mean? Oh, it's our man alright; I can feel it in my bones."

They reached the bustling centre of Celbridge. Once a quiet market town, in recent years it had been transformed into a commuter haven. It was nine thirty, and the wide main street was beginning to fill up. Cars and the odd tractor were parked on either side. People ambled along, stopping to chat. Kate wondered if the news had spread, the word that one of their own had been slain. It wasn't a common occurrence in places like this. The odd car crash, yes, even an occasional farmer putting a shotgun to his head, or a drunken brawl outside a pub. But not murder, in cold blood, not here.

"Roll down your window, will you," said Jim. "I'll pull in here. See if you can get exact directions to Monastery Road, it's somewhere out the far side of the town, but I don't want to piss about trying to find it."

Jim Corcoran had a hopeless sense of direction, she had lost count of the number of times they'd missed a turn-off or gone wildly astray, especially outside Dublin, and he hated the satnav. No sooner had they stopped than a portly man in a green apron bearing the words "Gino's Café" approached the car.

"Could you direct us to Monastery Road, please?"

"There's no shred of a monastery left if it's sightseeing you're after."

"Gino's" round face creased into a grin.

"No, we're not looking for the monastery, just the road."

Kate smiled back. Corcoran pushed the gearstick into first and revved the engine. The man took the hint.

"Go right down to the end of the town, past the secondary school and turn left after the basketball courts. That's Monastery Road; it stretches for about three miles out as far as Marystown."

Jim indicated right, stuck his arm out in a hand signal and pulled into the stream of traffic, oblivious to the annoyance of other drivers. Kate called a thank you towards the man. The secondary school was a series of single-storey buildings and a couple of Portakabins; Corcoran took the turn quickly. Monastery Road was narrow, with hedgerows and fields on both sides. Every few hundred yards there was a house. Most were big, newly built detached homes, which in Dublin would have cost a small fortune. They'd only driven about two miles when, around a bend bordered by high hedges, they reached the murder scene.

The McMahon home looked fairly new, a substantial detached dormer painted primrose-yellow, with large picture windows and a shiny slate roof. The drive rose slightly from the road, making the house seem quite imposing. It seemed like every Garda in Kildare was on the scene, from the number of squad cars parked in front of the house. The door was open, and an officer stood outside, cigarette in hand, quickly dropping it under his heel when he recognised their car. He spoke briefly into his radio and approached the two detectives as they were climbing into their scene of crime suits. Given that the local officers were in regular uniform, the crime scene was probably contaminated already, but Jim was a stickler for procedure, if only to make a point to the locals.

"DI Corcoran, DS Hamilton – Harcourt St," he snapped. "Who's in charge here?"

"Inspector Egan, sir."

"Bobby Egan?"

"Yes, sir. He's inside in the kitchen, at the back."

Jim pushed the front door open and stopped. Black and yellow tape criss-crossed a door to the left, but the hall was unremarkable in every other way. On the right was a table with a phone and a vase of dried flowers, on the left a mirrored coat stand laden with rubber boots, umbrellas and overcoats. On the walls pretty watercolours jostled with a large number of photos. Kate studied the pictures. There were two sons, close in age, both had graduated university, smiling in their black gowns, clutching degree parchments, as their parents looked on. Deirdre McMahon was a small dark-haired woman, attractive, with a penchant for smart colourful outfits, a different one for each occasion. The older boy had married recently, and the assembled clans beamed out from a classic group shot.

The polished wooden floor was clean and appeared print-free, but as the two officers made their way towards the back of the hall, they walked by the walls, just in case. The rear door opened before they reached it. A well-built fifty-something man in full forensic gear greeted them.

"Jim Corcoran, it's been far too long..."

"You're right, Bobby, and it's only bad news that brings us together."

"Nasty business alright, Jim; glad to have you around for this one." They shook hands, and Inspector Robert Egan ushered them towards a Garda mobile command unit parked outside.

"This is Sergeant Hamilton," said Jim. Kate shook the other man's hand, though it felt odd with her latex gloves against his own.

"I'll fill you in on what we know. Mind you, that's not very much, I'm afraid," said Egan, who had a broad accent that Kate thought might be from Donegal.

"Did you know the victim?" said Jim.

"I did, Jim. This is the sticks – we really do all know one another."

The two men smiled.

"Deirdre McMahon was well liked in these parts. She taught piano to half the kids in the town, including my two girls."

"And the husband?"

"I knew you'd ask me that next," said Egan. "He's not our man, I'd nearly swear to it. One of his golf partners was our desk sergeant for about thirty years. I spoke to him this morning at their hotel. They were out on the course all day;

then the four of them had dinner together and spent most of last night in the hotel bar. They all had a few too many, and it was at least four o'clock before they turned in. Hugh, the husband, was sharing a room with Ken, and Ken swears he didn't leave during the night."

"What's he like?"

"Quiet man, not a boozer that I know of. Been retired about two or three years."

"He was a teacher, wasn't he?"

"Yes, deputy head at first, then made headmaster a couple of years before he retired."

"Any kids?"

"Two boys, grown up now. One fella's in New York; the other lad's a solicitor in a big practice in Dublin. When we got hold of Hugh McMahon, he said he was going to contact his sons and break the bad news himself."

"OK, talk me through what happened this morning," said Jim.

Kate could see Corcoran was growing impatient. She felt it too; nothing Egan had said offered even a half-decent lead. The sooner they saw the victim, the sooner they could begin their own investigation.

"One of the sixth years from the local school had a lesson booked for nine o'clock..." said Egan.

"On a weekday?" asked Kate.

"Yes, she had time off from school for it. She's studying music for the Leaving Cert. The girl cycled up here."

"What happened then?"

"She rang the bell a couple of times and, when she didn't get an answer, went round the back. She's been coming here since she was knee-high, so she just pushed in the back door and called out for Deirdre."

"It wasn't locked?"

"No. When she didn't find her in the kitchen, young

Ashling decided to go through to the front room, where the piano is, and that's when she found the body."

"I think it's time we had a look for ourselves, don't you?" said Corcoran, standing up. "Is the girl still here?"

"Her mother came to collect her; we have a preliminary statement," said Egan. "I'll be talking to her again later. You can come along if you like."

"We'll probably stick around here till the pathologist arrives. Can we view the crime scene?" said Corcoran, and Egan led them into the house.

Egan stripped back some of the adhesive tape at the sitting room door, then stepped aside to let Jim Corcoran go in first. Kate clipped on her mask.

"Tell me you've preserved the scene, Bob?" said Corcoran wearily.

"I wasn't the first here, Jim. Two of our lads were running a speed trap down on the dual carriageway when the call came in. They got here first. They swear they didn't disturb anything. The room's been sealed since I had a look in about an hour ago."

"Who put the blanket over her?"

"The traffic lads did that. Not best practice, I know, and I gave them a bollocking for it, but you have to understand – both of them knew her," said Egan.

He looked embarrassed. Kate's heart sank; any fibre evidence on the body could well have been compromised by that simple gesture. Egan stayed in the hall; she followed her boss into the sitting room. It was a big, pleasant room, if a little cluttered. Deirdre McMahon was evidently fond of dried flowers. There were bowls and vases filled with lavish arrangements on the fireplace, the windowsills, the coffee table and on top of the upright piano, which graced the back wall. It gave the place a funereal feel, not least because of the still figure draped in a colourful throw and stretched sacrificially on the settee.

Kate had the impression of a "staging". Like some grotesque shop window display, the killer had left the murder scene prepared for whoever would find it. Only the covering of the body had disrupted his plan. Focusing her camera, she began to record the images, and felt the familiar dread in her stomach as Corcoran delicately removed the covering from Deirdre McMahon's lifeless form.

## 10

"Christ, you were right, boss," breathed Kate, hastily putting the camera to her eyes before the nausea welled up.

"I knew it was the same bastard; don't ask me how; I was just sure."

Corcoran crouched down beside Deirdre McMahon's final resting place; music teacher, wife and mother. Her head was propped up with a cushion, her eyes open and staring. She was semi-naked apart from the sheen of drying blood, which covered almost every shred of flesh, and what appeared to be the remains of pyjamas. Her hands were folded across her waist, doing little to cover the carnage that had been wrought on her slight frame. There were too many stab wounds to count, across her breasts and abdomen; they glistened in the watery sunlight from the picture window. Her face was untouched. Like a drowning swimmer, it floated white and ghostlike just above the tide of blood that had seeped through her nightclothes and into the fabric of the sofa. The two detectives were silent; only the click and whirr of Kate's camera sounded in the hushed room. She could hear her heart beating, and her mind was racing through the clues before her. The victim's age, the numerous stab wounds, the nightclothes. It *was* a pattern, wasn't it? Her first instinct on seeing Deirdre McMahon's body was to agree with Corcoran, but Kate was determined to keep an open mind. Let the evidence speak for itself.

"Do you think she was alive when he stabbed her?"

"It's hard to tell; there's more blood this time, a lot more; it looks to me like she was alive and the heart was still pumping for some of those wounds," said Corcoran.

"You're right; there's a significant splatter pattern around the couch, on the coffee table and on the carpet."

He nodded and continued a slow walk around the body.

"It looks like this is the main crime scene. There's no blood trail as far as I can see, so he must have attacked her while she was on the couch," he said. "It seems she didn't stand a chance, didn't even have the opportunity to get up or try to run."

It was a horrible thought. Small, pretty Deirdre McMahon, unable to fight back or escape. Kate played the scene in her mind's eye, the rise and fall of a gloved hand, the glint of steel penetrating soft flesh.

"Any sign of a weapon?" asked Corcoran.

"There's nothing here that looks likely; we'll have to check the kitchen. Did Harriet give you a description of the one used in the Connolly killing?"

"I spoke to her first thing this morning; she said we should be looking for a thin-bladed knife or even a spike of some sort, like a stiletto maybe," he said.

"A stiletto! Here? It's not exactly Mafia country. When have you seen a murder weapon like that?" said Kate.

"I know, it's very unusual, but that's what she said."

"When's she coming down?"

"She should be here before noon. With any luck we might

be able to get the body back to Dublin tonight or first thing in the morning."

Kate criss-crossed the room slowly, taking pictures. Corcoran seemed transfixed by the body. Suddenly the crunch of fast wheels on gravel set off a disturbance outside the house. Inspector Egan appeared in the open door.

"It's Hugh," he said, "the husband. He's arrived; what should we do?"

"Shut the door, Bob, for fuck's sake. That man will lose his mind if he sees her like this."

Kate went to the window. A short white-haired man stood just outside the porch. Bob Egan had moved outside quickly and was speaking intently to him, one hand holding on to his arm, partly, it seemed, to prevent him entering the house, partly as a gesture of sympathy. Hugh McMahon looked towards the room, shock and fear draining his face of colour. She felt compelled to nod to him, as though politeness would see them both through a situation so out of the ordinary. Then she went back to documenting the scene. Corcoran went to the door.

"I'd better go and talk to him. See if you can find a key for this room," he said, "at the very least put one of the local guards outside, and make sure no one enters until the Technical Bureau gets here."

Left alone in the sitting room, Kate put down the camera; there was nothing more to photograph. Now she had to confront her own weakness and look directly at the woman whose death had brought her here. Even in the midst of a violent end, shreds of a life lived were there to be noted. Although dressed for bed, the woman was still wearing make-up, a trace of lipstick remained on the slack mouth, and mascara was smudged around her eyes.

"You've been crying, haven't you?" said Kate, momentarily surprised at her own voice in the silence. Perhaps Deirdre had argued with her killer, pleaded for her life. As before, Kate knew the features of the victim and the visions they conjured up would take a long time to erase from her thoughts. Tearing her eyes from the ravaged corpse, she looked down at the coffee table. It was a two-tiered affair, with a magazine shelf underneath. On top lay an open magazine; it was either *OK!* or *Hello*. Next to it was a big bar of plain chocolate, half-eaten. Kate bagged and tagged it, along with the magazine.

*Were you just settling down to a relaxing evening on your own, or were you expecting a lover to call, waiting there with your make-up on, ready for bed?*

There were blood spatters on the open page of the magazine, crimson polka dots across the face of a minor starlet, her new baby clutched to her enhanced breasts. Kate felt a shiver run through her. The feeling was inescapable that this was precisely what the killer wanted. The flower arrangement on the coffee table seemed free of bloodstains. If that was so, and microscopic examination would be needed to confirm it, this meant the flowers had been placed there after the killing. Kate had learnt with the FBI that it was not uncommon for some serial killers to leave their victims posed. It was just another way of controlling both their victims and the law enforcement agencies out to catch them. Could this be the second murder of a potential serial killer?

The enormity of it all threatening to overwhelm her, Kate finally turned her back on the scene. As she entered the hall, the front door burst open to reveal the victim's husband, with both Bob Egan and Jim Corcoran trying to restrain him.

"Let me go, will you; I'm entitled to see her. This is my home, for God's sake," he said, his voice breaking.

Kate quickly closed the sitting room door and placed herself between the husband and the crime scene.

"Mr McMahon, please. That's really not a good idea," she

said, placing her hand on his chest, gently holding him back. "I promise you, we will allow you to see your wife, sir, but not here and not now."

Perhaps it was her touch or Kate's calm voice, but suddenly the man seemed to lose his strength, like air from a balloon, all forward momentum left him, and he allowed Egan and Corcoran to lead him back outside.

In the mobile unit Hugh McMahon collapsed onto a seat and put his head in his hands. The two men looked expectantly at Kate. Why was it always the female officers who got lumbered at times like this? She felt just as bad as they did. She sat beside the man, and the other two sat opposite. McMahon had gone from beetroot red and angry to a pallid grey. Kate was concerned he might have a heart attack; he was quite overweight and about the right age.

"Do you think we could have some hot sweet tea?" she asked.

Egan left to find someone to make the drink. Corcoran took out his notebook and cleared his throat.

"Mr McMahon, I realise you're very upset, but if you could compose yourself, I have to ask you some questions."

The man raised his head and looked blankly at Corcoran.

"I'm Detective Inspector Jim Corcoran of the Murder Squad, sir. I've come down from Dublin for the investigation. Do you think you could answer some questions for me?"

Gradually the man's face formed itself into a semblance of attention, and he nodded.

"When did you last see your wife, sir?"

Shakily, McMahon outlined his movements. He'd left Kildare with three friends on the previous Saturday and, until that morning, had been staying in one of Wexford's smarter golf resorts.

"So you saw her last on Saturday?"

"Yes, Deirdre got up early to see me off. It must have been

about seven. We had a cup of coffee; then she was going back for a lie-in."

"Have you spoken to your wife since then?"

"Yes of course. I always ring home when I'm away."

"How often did you ring?"

"Every day."

"Tell me about those conversations, starting with Saturday."

"Oh God, I can't remember exactly," said McMahon. "Just the usual. I rang to say we'd arrived safely. We weren't on for long."

"Can you remember what she said?"

"Nothing really, nothing."

"Try to remember; did she mention any plans?"

"Just one of those meaningless conversations people have."

He paused; they waited.

"She said she'd been into town. She bought some shoes." He said the word "shoes" like it was an illicit substance. The inflection didn't go unnoticed.

"Go on," said Kate.

"We had," he said, "we had words about it." Hugh McMahon pushed his fingers through thinning hair.

"Deirdre has dozens of shoes. I swear there must be a hundred pairs – none of them cheap either."

He looked at Kate, as if it was something she would understand. McMahon shifted awkwardly in his chair.

"I just don't understand why she had to have so many." His tone had become defensive. "It's not like she can ever wear them all."

"Did you argue?" asked Corcoran.

"No. No, we didn't argue, exactly. I just said I thought it was a bit, well, a bit excessive. It's not two weeks since she bought the last pair."

"So you had a bit of a tiff..."

Corcoran's voice was sympathetic, even soothing. Kate kept her head down, allowing her boss to build a rapport. The man's hands were clenching and unclenching on the table.

"I suppose you could call it that. She can be so exasperating. She said, 'It's my money. I'll spend it how I like.' It's her answer to everything – you know what I mean?"

Corcoran nodded. *That's right*, thought Kate, *give him enough rope.*

"How did the call finish?"

"I hung up on her. She started on about my golf, the amount of time I spend on it, the money it costs. I just lost patience."

"You lost patience."

Corcoran left the words hanging. Kate took up the chase.

"Did you often lose patience with your wife?"

"No, no, of course not. Not often. We had words now and then; for God's sake, we've been married thirty years, who doesn't?"

"Did you ring her back?"

"No, not then. I called last night though."

"And...?"

"I didn't apologise, if that's what you're asking. She was cool with me."

"What time was this?"

"About six-ish, when we came back in from our second round."

"What do you mean, cool?" said Kate.

"Oh, I don't know." Exasperation showed in his face. "Deirdre and I have these spats all the time; usually it blows over."

"Was there something different this time?"

"I'd kind of forgotten about the shoes and the row. I'd had

a really good round, my best ever." He sighed heavily. "I wanted to tell her about it."

"Did you tell her?"

"I did. She said nothing."

"Did she refer to your row?"

"No. She barely spoke. I was sorry I rang. We said good-night, and I went to the bar."

Kate was fighting a growing dislike of Hugh McMahon. She knew he was probably typical of his generation, pompous and self-centred, if not downright chauvinistic. But could he have something to do with the murder despite his alibi?

A knock on the van door interrupted them. It was the Garda they'd first met at the front door.

"Two officers from the Technical Bureau have just arrived, sir."

Kate stood up.

"Shall I go?" she said.

"Yes, we'll head back to Dublin shortly and leave them to it. They'll start outside and work their way in. They can tell the local team to suit up and help. I'll finish up here with Mr McMahon," said Corcoran.

As she went to meet the Technical Bureau chief who'd just emerged from his car, one of the local officers stopped Kate.

"I didn't want to interrupt, but I thought you should see this."

With latex-gloved hands he gave her a sheaf of newspapers encased in a polythene evidence bag. Kate was able to see that the bunch included every single one of Tuesday's daily papers, both broadsheet and tabloid. In each case the pages were open on the report of Irene Connolly's murder.

"Where did these come from?"

"They were on the front seat of McMahon's car."

"And you just took them out? Did he give you permission to search his car?"

The young officer had the good grace to look embarrassed.

"No, Sergeant...I didn't exactly ask. He got out of the car and left the door open when Inspector Egan came to meet him. I know Mr McMahon; he taught me in school. I just went over to offer my condolences. Then I went to shut the car door. That's when I saw the newspapers."

Kate was equally annoyed and excited. If, *and it was a very big if*, McMahon was tried for the murders, a good defence lawyer could have the "evidence", such as it was, thrown out of court because it was seized without a warrant.

"Let's hope this doesn't come back to bite us, Guard," said Kate. "For fuck's sake, you should know better."

Keeping the evidence bag, she walked away from the officer. *Could McMahon have murdered both women?* At the very least it established a connection between the victims, and might just make the grieving widower a viable suspect.

"Would you mind briefing the techies?" she said to Inspector Egan, who was shaking hands with the senior technical officer. "I need to show these to DI Corcoran."

"I take it Jim wants them to start now?"

"Yes. He also wants your guys to suit up and help with the search. We'll vacate the scene now for them to start."

She turned back to the mobile unit, excitement building in her stomach, wondering how best to let Corcoran know this potentially explosive new information. Outside the door of the van, she could hear McMahon's whiney voice.

"A teacher's pension is nowhere near enough these days."

"Sir!"

One look and Corcoran stood.

"Bear with me, Mr McMahon. I need to talk to Sergeant

Hamilton for a moment," he said and stepped outside, closing the sliding door behind him.

Kate handed him the newspapers without a word.

"Jesus Christ! Where did these come from?"

"McMahon's car, front seat."

Corcoran allowed himself a smile.

"Well, well, well, I think I might just have another little chat with Hugh."

"Here?"

"No. Let's give Forensics some space. I think we should get our man up to Dublin, don't you?"

Kate took the papers to her car to be entered into evidence. Corcoran turned back to the mobile unit, a new purpose in his movements.

"Mr McMahon," he said, "I need you to remove the clothes you are wearing, place them in these bags and put on this suit. It's a routine procedure; I'm sure you'll understand."

Hugh McMahon looked irritated by the request, and it seemed as if he might argue. Then Kate told him he would be brought to Dublin for questioning. His annoyance seemed to evaporate. He just looked a little pathetic. As he removed his golf sweater, Kate and Corcoran left the unit, leaving Egan to supervise the collection of the chief suspect's clothes.

# 11

DECEMBER 1967

The Jacksons made a brave attempt to celebrate Christmas as normal. Rosie's swollen belly meant that none of their regular guests could be invited. Old friends were put off with the story that she had the highly contagious scarlet fever. Sean and Marina spared no expense. The house was bedecked with more decorations than ever before. The twelve-foot spruce tree in the sitting room groaned with baubles and lights, and underneath was an array of presents piled high. Rosie had never seen so many, not even when she was small and still believed in Santa. She couldn't help but feel a little excited, and she clung to that childish thrill rather than let herself think past December 25.

In the kitchen she and her mother spent hours at the pine table, preparing Christmas fare. Neither mentioned the fact that there would be just the three of them to eat it all. Ever since she was small, standing on a chair to stir the big yellow mixing bowl, Rosie had loved to cook with her mother. Now, after a gap of a year or two when it had seemed too childish to Rosie, stuck in the house for days on end, she and her

mother had rediscovered that pleasure. If the hours of chop-
ping and mixing seemed a little excessive, and their enthu-
siasm a little frantic, mother and daughter said nothing to
disturb the bubble of activity.

It was not an easy pregnancy. Already at less than six
months, her belly was grossly swollen, she could not stand
for long, and her face was often flushed. Dr Magnier had
looked concerned on her last check-up after taking her blood
pressure, but he had refused to be drawn by her mother's
anxious questions.

"Nothing to worry about, my dear, but we do need to get
her settled into St Mary's very soon, the sooner the better,
really, so that we can keep a close eye on her."

Magnier did not like making house calls and had been
more than surprised when the Jacksons insisted on keeping
their daughter with them when her condition was so obvious.
Rosie had pleaded to be allowed to spend Christmas at home.
Ever since the first appointment with Magnier, when her
mother had told her that there wouldn't be any kind of operation, that instead she would spend weeks, even months
locked away in a convent, the thought of St Mary's had terrified Rosie. While Sean was away on business, and before she
got too big, Rosie and her mum had taken the bus to Donnybrook to look up at the forbidding walls of the convent. From
the gateway all they could see was the curving drive, a steep
rooftop and some willows. No visible sign of the inhabitants.

When the prospect of staying within the high walls came
to mind, Rosie was overcome with a panic she fought to hide.
For her own good, they said. To get through the ordeal as
quietly as possible, they said. To get back to her old self. No
matter how often the words were said, not one of them truly
believed them. It was just something they all repeated, to
keep from going mad.

No one talked about the baby. They talked of Rosie's

"accident", not her rape, her "condition", not her pregnancy, and the stay at St Mary's had become known as her "retreat". It was only in the depths of the night, when each believed the others were asleep, that Sean, Marina, and most of all Rosie, allowed the truth to surface and the tears to flow.

After all the preparations, Christmas Day was a let-down. While her parents attended nine-thirty Mass, Rosie went through her presents. The parcels, which had seemed so enticing, did little to thrill her once opened. All of the expensive clothes her mother had so lovingly chosen were for after her "retreat", so there was no joy in trying them on now. The records and books, which she would normally adore, seemed silly and childish. Her dad had bought her a transistor radio, her first, but any pleasure in it was tempered by the knowledge that he had chosen it with St Mary's in mind. The three of them ate dinner at two o'clock, the table laden with enough to feed ten people. Sean and Marina had drunk a couple of sherries beforehand, and even a casual observer would have noted that they were both more interested in the wine than the food. Rosie noticed the glitter in her mother's eyes, and her father's over-hearty laughter at the jokes from a whole box of crackers he insisted on sharing. As she toyed with the pile of food on her plate, all Rosie could think of was the suitcase her mother had packed, the one that would go with her to St Mary's in less than twenty-four hours.

After dinner Sean fell asleep in his armchair, a brandy by his side. Marina insisted on doing all the washing up herself while her daughter watched, achingly conscious that they would be parted soon, perhaps forever. The thought had taken root in her mind that the creature that kicked so fiercely within her would not be born without a mighty struggle, one Rosie was sure she couldn't survive.

St Stephen's Day dawned grey and wet. Rosie made her morning routine last twice as long as usual, lingering in the

bath her mother had run. Lying in the steamy warmth
scented with new bubble bath from her overstuffed
Christmas stocking, she stared at the white mound of her
stomach rising above the foam. Not for the first time she
closed her eyes and wished it gone, wished that she had
never met her handsome, cruel cousin, wished above all to
turn back the clock to a time when being with a boy was still
something mysterious and exciting.

Taking the sponge, she squeezed hot water onto her belly,
then watched amazed as a ripple of movement crossed her
pale stretched skin. She filled the sponge and did it again;
this time a bump appeared and moved slowly towards her
ribs. Despite herself she giggled. She tried the sponge a few
times more, but the water was cooling, and she wondered if
perhaps the baby couldn't feel the heat any more through her
skin. Or maybe it was asleep.

This was the first time she had felt that the horrible
swelling of her body, which had caused such hurt and worry,
which had changed her life so drastically, this thing, this
disaster, was a baby, a little person, inside her, growing and
feeling, waiting to come out.

"Rosie love, are you alright?"

"Yes, Mum, I'll be out in a minute."

"Right so, I'll see you downstairs. Daddy's put the stuff in
the car. We have to make a move soon."

Marina's voice had a catch in it. Awkwardly Rosie heaved
herself out of the water. She had to sit on the toilet seat to dry
herself. Eventually, she was dressed. Her mother had bought
her all the latest maternity styles, but the frumpy clothes
made Rosie want to weep.

In the kitchen her parents sat grim-faced over their coffee.
Marina jumped up, her face fixed in a brittle smile.

"What do you fancy, love, bacon and egg?"

"I'll just have some tea, Mum."

"You must have something to eat; what about cereal?"

Rosie gave in to please her. The cornflakes tasted of nothing, and she had trouble getting through even half a bowl, but she made them last. Then she asked for some toast, which killed another fifteen minutes. Finally, her father stood up.

"Right, young ladies, time to go," he said, almost achieving a jovial tone, earning him a tragic glare from his wife.

All too soon, after a silent journey through empty roads, Sean Jackson pulled the car in and stopped with the bonnet just a foot or two from the gates of St Mary's. A slightly built young man appeared and removed the padlock, then pushed back each gate in turn. He seemed to be expecting them. He didn't look into the car or ask what their business was. As they drew up to the front of the grey stone building, the door opened, and a tall thin nun came out. She didn't come down but waited to speak until the Jacksons had climbed up the twelve steps.

"Mr and Mrs Jackson, please follow me."

Her eyes did not meet theirs, and she barely glanced at Rosie. For what seemed like miles the little group trudged along dark wood-panelled corridors, up several flights of stairs until, finally, just when Rosie thought she might actually faint, the nun stopped at a door, identical to dozens they had passed, and knocked. The Jacksons heard no response, but she opened the door and led them inside.

"Please come in and sit down."

A diminutive figure stood up from behind a vast polished desk and smiled. Three high-backed chairs were arranged in front of the desk, and Sean helped his daughter into the middle one, waiting till Marina and the tiny nun were seated before taking his own place. Their escort had all but vanished, so silent was her exit. Rosie felt dizzy and was glad to rest her swollen ankles. There was a heavy scent in the air, a mixture of carbolic soap and musty books. Between the smell and pure fear, she couldn't concentrate.

"I am Mother Claire, Superior of St Mary's; there are some formalities to go through before you leave Rosemary with us."

"It's Rose actually, or Rosie..."

Marina Jackson's voice faltered, and her cold grip tightened on her daughter's hand.

"Rose-mary is the more usual form in Catholic baptism, for our Blessed Lady. You must forgive my error."

The polite smile did not extend to the nun's eyes. Marina didn't speak again. What followed seemed to be mostly concerned with bills to be paid, in guineas, in advance. Rosie's head was spinning. Only by concentrating on a speck on her new black patent shoes did she manage to keep from passing out. Her father said little, just nodding or giving monosyllabic answers. Then he signed some forms and handed over an envelope he took from his overcoat pocket. The nun gave him a receipt and put the envelope in a desk drawer.

"Is Dr Magnier here?" Sean asked.

"On St Stephen's Day? Dear me no, we're not expecting Professor Magnier to visit until after the New Year."

"But what about Rosie's medical care? Is there another doctor here?"

"I assure you, Mr Jackson, the girl will get whatever medical attention she needs. We have trained nursing sisters on duty twenty-four hours a day."

At that, the Mother Superior rose from behind the desk. The thin nun appeared at the door. Sean stood up, his shoulders sagging. Marina helped Rosie to her feet.

"I'll let you say your goodbyes here, in privacy," said

Mother Claire, "then Sister Walter will take your daughter to her room."

During the entire meeting, she had never once looked at Rosie or addressed her directly. The door closed soundlessly. Rosie was so overcome she had to sit down again, and, as soon as Marina bent to hug her, they were both in tears. Sean took out his handkerchief but found he needed it himself. A handbell sounded within the dark recesses of the building.

"She'll be back in a minute, love; we'd better say goodbye."

Marina straightened up, wiping her wet cheeks with the back of her hand.

"You'll come to see me, Mum, won't you?"

"We'll be in as often as they'll let us," said her father.

As they hugged one last time, the thin nun slipped back into the room. Rosie clung on for a moment; then seeing the frown of her escort over Marina's shoulder, she let go. Her mother's face was ashen, and tears had streaked her make-up. Sean put an arm around his wife and led her from the room, turning at the door to say, "Bye, love," and mouth a kiss. As their footsteps sounded down the corridor, the nun spoke.

"Pick up that case, Rose Mary, and follow me."

## 12

Hugh McMahon had never been inside a Dublin police station before, and it showed. Corcoran could have spared him the experience, but it was not his intention to make the man feel comfortable or relaxed. They had travelled to Harcourt Street with the portable blue light flashing on the roof of the unmarked vehicle. Occasionally, at traffic black spots, Corcoran had switched on the siren. At Garda HQ, they used the main station doorway rather than the more discreet side entrance.

In the porch sat an elderly vagrant wrapped in a filthy sleeping bag. He was a regular. On wintry days the desk sergeant tolerated him, even giving him the odd cup of tea. As long as he didn't bring in alcohol, ask for money, or smell. If he did start to stink, the sergeant would send him packing to the nearest hostel for a shower, but he always came back. He told anyone who would listen that the homeless shelters were too dangerous, with their druggies and drunks.

McMahon looked appalled to find himself in such company. Kate guided him through the front hall and took him straight to an interview room.

"I don't understand why you have brought me here. Surely I could have stayed in my own home."

He sounded both anxious and angry.

"Sir, your house is now a major crime scene; it will be some days before you can go back," said Kate.

"But where will I go?"

"I'm sure you'll be able to stay with friends, or there's your son."

"Oh my God, Tony! He's on his way home; he was leaving straight away, just after we put the phone down."

Kate and Corcoran exchanged looks. The son was a solicitor; the longer it took him to reach his father, the more time they had to question their one and only suspect.

"Don't worry, sir, the local officers will inform him of your whereabouts once he arrives in Celbridge" said Corcoran.

"But I should ring him, tell him to come here," said McMahon anxiously.

He began to pat his pockets, then remembered he was wearing the police boiler suit.

"My mobile, the number's on my mobile phone. You took it, with the rest of my stuff. Can't I just ring him and stop him going all the way down there for nothing?"

Kate took out her own phone and handed it to him.

"Your personal effects are with our Technical Bureau. Here, use my phone if you wish to call him."

He looked at the phone and keyed in the numbers zero eight seven; then he stopped. "It's no use, I have no idea what the number is; it's saved on my phone. I don't know it off by heart."

He slumped into one of the chairs, handing Kate back her phone without making eye contact. Corcoran sat on the far side of the small bare table. There was a tape recorder and several blank cassettes on a shelf. Kate loaded one, clicked the record button and, speaking slowly, gave the date, time and location.

"Detective Inspector Corcoran," said Jim.

"Detective Sergeant Hamilton," said Kate.

They both looked expectantly at McMahon. A tiny red light blinked on the tape recorder. He stared back vacantly.

"Please state your name for the recording," said Kate.

"Hugh McMahon," he said, his voice betraying nervousness.

"Mr McMahon, how do you know Irene Connolly?" asked Corcoran.

The man's jaw dropped.

"I don't know her, not really. I've never met her."

"We found the newspapers in your car," said Kate.

"Each one open on the report of her murder," said Corcoran.

"Deirdre knew her; they were friends," said McMahon.

"She was your wife's friend, but you never met her?"

"No, and I had no interest in meeting her either."

*There's that peevish tone again*, thought Kate.

"Why's that?"

He hesitated before answering.

"She moved in different circles to us. She and Deirdre only met up once a year, if that. That woman had nothing in common with us. I don't know why they persisted with the friendship."

"How did they come to be friends if, as you say, she moved in different circles?"

"They worked together, years ago, before Deirdre and I were married."

"What sort of work?"

"Aer Lingus, they worked for Aer Lingus back in the sixties. Deirdre lived in Dublin then. When we got married, she couldn't stay on, of course. Flitting all over the world like that, well, it was hardly appropriate for a teacher's wife; she stayed home with the boys."

"But the two kept in touch?"

"Yes, on and off. We didn't have two cars back then. Deirdre didn't get up to town much. Irene was married herself, living the high life. I didn't see the point of keeping in touch, but Deirdre carried on writing, and she'd get the odd postcard from abroad."

"Didn't you ever meet up as a foursome?" asked Kate.

"Oh, it was suggested alright, but I wasn't keen."

"Why?"

"Well," said McMahon, with some annoyance, "we were struggling financially. A teacher's pay was barely enough to live on. We were trying to buy our first house, and there *they* were in some mansion. I wasn't going to be patronised by any bloody lawyer and his snobby wife."

"You didn't like her much, did you?"

"I told you I never met the woman!"

"So what made you think she was snobby?"

"I just knew."

"How did you know, Mr McMahon?"

"From Deirdre, things she said. Irene was always filling her head full of nonsense. Whenever they met up, I'm telling you – no good came of it. Deirdre would come home, and I would bear the brunt of it."

"How do you mean?"

"Oh, I don't know...She'd be on my back over every little thing. She went to the house once, the big bloody pile in Killiney. When she came home, there was hell to pay! Nothing was good enough anymore, her clothes, our home, nothing. We had a little cottage in the town then. It wasn't much, but it was the best we could get on my wages. After seeing Irene's house, Deirdre was miserable for months."

"Did you argue about Irene, about their friendship?"

"Damn right we argued. What was I supposed to do, rob a bank? That Liam Connolly was born with a silver spoon; he might have been a barrister but only because his father was before him. He inherited the whole thing, the house, the law firm – the lot! I had to work for anything we had, bloody hard too. Standing up in front of a class full of ungrateful, spotty brats every day for the best part of forty years is no fucking picnic! Deirdre couldn't see how unfair she was being. She wanted what Irene had, and when I couldn't give it to her, it made her dissatisfied with me and what we had."

"Yet she kept up the friendship?"

"Yes."

"For all these years?"

"Yes."

"And still you never met Irene?"

"No, I tell you, I never met her, nor did I wish to."

"So why the newspapers, why buy them all, why read them all?"

"I was interested, that's all." McMahon looked cagey.

"Interested in the death of a woman you didn't like and had never met?" said Corcoran.

"Yes," he said, "it's not every day someone you're... acquainted with gets murdered."

"No – yet two women you know have been murdered in the last three days," said Corcoran.

McMahon looked like he'd been slapped.

"I want to see my son," he said shakily.

"He's a lawyer, isn't he? Might come in handy."

"I'm not going to answer any more questions until Tony gets here."

McMahon's mouth clamped shut once the words were out. Kate went back to the tape machine.

"Interview with Mr Hugh McMahon suspended at 15.26; DS Hamilton and DI Corcoran leaving the interview room."

She clicked the off switch and turned back to the table.

"We will try to make contact with your son, Mr McMahon. In the meantime, would you like a tea or coffee?"

Abruptly, the man stood up and headed towards the door.

"I don't have to stay here, do I? I'm not under arrest."

"No, you're not under arrest," said Corcoran from the doorway. "However, we do have some more questions for you, and I believe it would be in your best interests to remain here for the moment until we can clear them up."

"Why should I? You've taken my clothes, made me wear this ridiculous thing" – he tugged at the flimsy boiler suit angrily – "and you refuse to let me telephone my son."

"Not at all, sir," said Kate. "You are of course free to call your son at any time. You were simply unable to recall his number."

She went on in a more soothing tone.

"Let me get you a hot drink and maybe a sandwich, and I'll see if I can get in touch with the Celbridge Gardai and locate Tony."

She placed a hand on his upper arm and guided him back to his seat. "You don't want to be wandering the city in this, do you?" she said, indicating the suit.

"No, I suppose not." He sat down heavily. "I don't want any food, just a cup of tea."

"Fine, I'll send someone along with it."

The two detectives left him. Outside, Kate ordered the tea from a passing clerk, and they headed for her boss's office.

"Well, what do you think?" asked Corcoran.

"He certainly didn't like the first victim, that's for sure," said Kate, "and it doesn't sound like the happiest of marriages either."

"But? There's a 'but' coming, isn't there," said Corcoran.

"But...he still doesn't strike me as the murdering type."

"Shit! I knew you were going to say that."

"I'm not saying he's not our man!" said Kate. "It's just..."

"I know, I know," said Corcoran, running his fingers through his unruly hair, "he's a whining little weasel, but he's not an axe murderer, is he?"

"Not as far as I can tell. But he has given us something very important, sir, a link between the two victims."

"Bloody right he has. It's got to be the same killer. And I bet you anything Forensics confirm it."

"We won't have anything definitive from Kildare for days yet," said Kate. "In the meantime..."

"In the meantime let's put some more pressure on our prime suspect," said Corcoran. "He might be an unlikely candidate, but he's all we've got."

"He has to know something that will help us," said Kate, following him down the corridor towards the lift. Corcoran stabbed a finger at the call button.

"We'll get him printed; we'll take a DNA swab. You check out his alibi again; you've got the names of his golf partners and the hotel," he said. "Get statements over the phone, and make sure they know we'll follow them up for written accounts. If his alibi is not watertight for every minute since he left Kildare, especially in the early hours when the others were asleep, I want to know it."

The lift doors slid open to reveal an officer from the front office accompanied by a man in his mid-twenties. He was dressed formally in a navy suit, white shirt and blue tie.

"Ah, sir, this is Tony McMahon," said the Garda.

For an instant they all froze, the two inside the lift hesitant to leave, Kate and Corcoran both mentally working out if they should give Tony immediate access to his father or attempt to stall him.

"I'm very sorry for your loss," said Kate, offering her hand. The lift doors began to close, but Corcoran stepped into the gap and nudged them back with his shoulder. Tony

McMahon gripped her hand. Kate felt sorry for him. His mother had died in horrific circumstances, and now his father was in custody, a suspect.

"Let's go to my office," said Corcoran, leading the way.

Once inside Corcoran's office, he introduced himself and Kate, shook hands with Tony and offered his condolences. The young lawyer, dark-haired like his late mother, had even features, an attractive face and a slight, almost boyish build. Tony McMahon looked like he should still be in college, not acting on behalf of a murder suspect.

"I understand you are holding my father; what the hell is going on?"

"We are not holding your father," said Kate, pulling out a chair for him. "We simply need to interview him, and the house is undergoing a technical examination."

Tony sat wearily.

"I know, I went there after he called to tell me...They wouldn't let me in. Not even to see Mum..."

His voice faltered, and he struggled for a moment to compose himself.

"Inspector Egan told me she'd been stabbed, is that true?" he asked.

"Yes, I'm afraid that seems to be the case."

The youthful face contorted, and Tony looked at the floor, clenching and unclenching his hands.

"Can I get you some water?" said Kate.

"Do you know if she suffered..." Tony said. "You know, do you think she was aware...that she knew what was happening?"

His eyes were tortured.

"There's really no way of knowing yet," said Corcoran.

After a moment Kate spoke.

"Tony, we're going to have to ask you some questions, just

routine enquiries, but it might be best to get it over with now."

She didn't add "before you see your father".

"What about my father?"

"He's just having a cup of tea," said Corcoran. "You can join him as soon as we've taken your statement."

"How is he?"

It seemed to Kate that the question was asked not so much out of concern but curiosity. A look at her boss confirmed that he'd heard the same edge in Tony McMahon's voice.

"He's bearing up," she said, "under the circumstances."

Again, there was a flicker of something interesting on Tony's face. Anger, maybe.

"There's an interview room this way, sir; shall we get it over with?"

Corcoran left them to it. Kate knew he was going back to talk to McMahon Senior. Even as she prepared another blank cassette to record the testimony of the victim's youngest son, Kate doubted whether either man held the key to the murders. If she was right, they could be wasting valuable time, time that the killer could use to cover his tracks or plan his next violent act.

# 13

26 DECEMBER 1967

Rosie's room at St Mary's was little more than a cell. By the time she had carried her case up the final flight of stairs to the top floor, she was close to collapse. It had been weeks since she could tackle such strenuous effort easily. Now she was red-faced and panting. The nun gave no quarter, barely slowing her pace when Rosie lagged behind. Stopping at an unmarked door, she opened it with a key from her belt and ushered Rosie inside. Finally she spoke.

"Keep your room clean and tidy at all times, no personal effects on show, no food or drinks, no smoking, no cosmetics or perfumes allowed. You may be subject to inspection at any hour of the day or night. Lunch is at twelve thirty; you may unpack and put away your belongings and rest quietly until then. You'll find a prayer book beside your bed."

"Thank you, Sister," said Rosie.

She dragged her case the last few feet into the room and turned to find herself alone and apparently locked in. Wrestling with the doorknob amid rising panic, she finally wrenched open the door, and a blonde girl tumbled in and almost sprawled on the dark parquet floor. She giggled, then put a hand across her mouth to stifle the noise.

"Bloody lock's as stiff as anything; did you really think Wally Dom had locked you in?"

"Yes, just for a moment."

"They might as well lock the doors, feckin' witches, for all the freedom we get!" Rosie's visitor plonked down on the bed and patted the space beside her.

"Holy God, you'd better sit down; you look awful!"

Rosie didn't argue. The narrow bed creaked under them. She felt it was probably her weight doing the most damage.

"Bernie Murphy, at your service."

"Rosie Jackson, at yours."

Again they giggled. Rosie couldn't believe that just minutes from crying like her heart might break, she was laughing. It felt almost the same. She wondered if this was hysteria. Bernie patted Rosie's bump gently.

"When are you due?"

It was the first time Rosie had spoken about her pregnancy to anyone but her parents; it felt very odd.

"I'm not sure," she admitted, a little embarrassed. "They haven't told me exactly when it will...em...happen."

"I've got sixteen weeks to go, there or thereabouts," said Bernie, "but you're a good bit bigger than me, so you must be nearly ready to pop!"

Rosie's heart sank; the notion of being "ready to pop" was terrifying.

"You seem to know a lot about...all this," she said.

"I have five brothers and sisters younger than me," said Bernie. "I've seen it all five times over."

Rosie couldn't imagine being one of six children.

"Don't you know how to calculate your dates?" asked her new friend.

"Not a clue."

"Easy, you count forty weeks from the last time you had the curse."

Rosie's face flushed deep red. The "curse" – did everyone here know about the awful night with Richard? Bernie sensed her discomfort.

"The curse is your monthly, you know, your period," she said. Rosie attempted a smile, pretending she'd known what it meant.

"I only ever had a couple of periods. I'd hardly started them when...this happened."

"How old are you?" asked Bernie.

"Fourteen and a half; how old are you?"

"Holy God, you're the youngest here. I'm eighteen in June. I'm getting married on my birthday; me and my fella are going to run away together, to Gretna Green, that's in Scotland."

Rosie looked at her companion in amazement, but before she could ask any more questions, a single bell sounded, and Bernie pushed herself up off the bed. She reached out a hand to pull Rosie up too.

"Dinner time. Thank God above in Heaven, I'm bloody starving. Come on, Rosie Jackson, let's see what muck they've got for us today."

There were seven around the refectory table, not counting the nun. She sat at the head, having led the girls in grace while they stood, heads bowed, beside their chairs. Lunch consisted of tomato soup, followed by stew made with a meat Rosie couldn't identify. It might have been mutton or beef. She surprised herself by eating a fair bit. There was dessert too, a very sticky lump of Christmas pudding smothered in thick custard. Rosie didn't like it. She longed for her mother's wonderful plum pudding, its dark golden sponge speckled with sweet fruit. They had made it many weeks before Christmas, taking turns to make a wish as they stirred the mixture. Rosie blinked back tears as she remembered her wish.

In an effort to take her mind off home, she looked around her at the other girls. Bernie was on her right, scraping the last of the custard from her bowl. When it was bare, she looked longingly at Rosie's untouched pudding. Discreetly Rosie slid the bowl over and took the empty one. Bernie grinned and plunged her spoon into the congealing mess. On Rosie's left sat a girl whom she thought must be at least twenty. She was broad shouldered with a big mass of curly black hair pinned back untidily, and an apple-cheeked face. Rosie put her down as a countrywoman, for no other reasons than her freckly arms and rosy complexion. Four girls sat opposite, ranging in age from about eighteen to twenty-five. After another prayer, they were dismissed by the thin nun, who went by the name of Walter Dominic. Rosie followed the other girls from the refectory. The line trooped quietly along a panelled corridor. Rosie was losing her bearings, but she kept close to her new friend as the girls filed into a big room full of heavy, dark furniture.

It seemed that they were supposed to observe silence, but Bernie whispered that this was the Parlour, and led Rosie to a seat near the open fire. Each of the girls got a cotton bag from a shelf and settled down to rummage inside. Some took out knitting needles and wool and tiny bits of cardigans. Others were working on embroidered cot sheets or crochet shawls. The thin nun took Rosie to a large cupboard.

"You can choose, Rose Mary. Do you want to knit, sew or crochet some useful item for your unfortunate child?"

Rosie was mortified and could only stare at the bag in her hand. It was embroidered with the name Catherine in one corner.

"Can you knit, girl?" The nun was becoming impatient.

"Yes, Sister," said Rosie.

She gave her some needles and a ball of soft yellow wool.

"Get Agnes to show you what to do," she said; then she was gone. Rosie looked round, confused; which one was Agnes?

Bernie smiled and waved her over.

"Who's Agnes?" Rosie whispered, though the other girls were chatting happily, if quietly, now that the nun was gone.

"It's me, silly. I told you we all had convent names. Even though Bernadette is a saint's name, I'm only bringing shame on it, so in here I'm Agnes."

"Well, Agnes, what do I do? Is there a pattern for this thing I have to knit?"

"Call me Bernie unless the witches are listening. Cast on forty-two stitches, then knit one plain one purl for twelve rows."

The five other girls had gathered round, and Bernie made the introductions. It was very confusing because of the convent names. Everyone insisted on telling her their real name.

"You're so lucky; they more or less let you keep your real name and just tacked on a Mary for holiness," said the curly-haired one who had been next to Rosie at dinner. She had a broad Kerry accent. While the others were eager to talk about their homes and families, Rosie kept her personal information to a minimum. She told the others she was from Dublin and had no brothers or sisters. She soon realised that she was the youngest of them all, by a good two years, but she had almost the biggest bump despite the fact that two of the girls, Annie/Elizabeth and Deirdre/Claire, were nearly due.

Their craft session lasted two hours, and Rosie was surprised by how much she enjoyed it. In the six months since that fateful night in July, her whole world had shrunk to four walls. Home had started to feel like a prison. She missed her friends and the hustle and bustle of school. Now, for a brief while, among strangers, she was oddly content.

# 14

Billy Butler and his new lodger shared the old building companionably. They didn't get under each other's feet because the American was out most of the time, so Billy simply reverted to his routine. The evening that the visitor moved in, they went to the pub at about nine. On the small TV over the bar, the national news headlined the story of a second baffling murder in a few days. The handful of midweek regulars around the bar shook their heads and murmured. Their voices only rose with excitement when the sports news came on. Billy paid no attention to the TV. The nuns had preferred radio for their limited connection to the outside world, so he had no taste for television. World events passed him by. He liked music and turned on the radio every day for a bit of noise and company. Now, of course, he had some real company. The American had a way of drawing him out, and Billy was getting used to the pleasure of talking and of having someone listen.

"You must have met a lot of people over the years, Billy; tell me about them."

"Oh, I did indeed, hundreds of them. All girls and nuns,

mind you, not that many men. Only the doctors and priests were men, of course, and sometimes the Sunday visitors."

"The Sunday visitors?"

"That was the only day they were allowed to come, on Sunday afternoons. Only some of them, mind...many's the girl never had no one."

"Was this the nuns or the patients who had callers?"

Billy looked blankly at his companion.

"Patients?" he said.

"The girls, I mean the girls."

"Sister Ursula had a brother who used to come now and again."

"And the girls, they had visitors every Sunday?"

"Some did, some didn't. Them that didn't cried a lot. So did them that *had* the visitors. God almighty, the weeping there was when their mammies left them."

Billy's eyes stared into the distance. The American had quickly learned to wait for the old man's memories to surface, though it pained him.

"That place was a vale of tears alright. There never was a day back then when I didn't see someone bawling their eyes out."

Billy had a disconcerting habit of quoting from scripture and hymns in the oddest places; it irritated his companion, reminding him of his childhood.

"That must have been tough on you, buddy."

"When I was a young fella, it used to upset me. Tell you the truth, when I first came to St Mary's, I did a fair bit of crying meself."

"You were just a kid."

"The nuns didn't like it though, not in a boy. They didn't mind the girls crying one little bit, but I wasn't supposed to. Not even when they slapped me."

"They beat you?"

"Oh, they did alright. Not as bad as the Christian Brothers. The sisters never used a leather or a cane on me, but they'd give you a wallop on the back of the neck or a slap on the hand as soon as look at you." The old man rubbed his broad palms together and smiled. "D'ya know it's funny, but them pure white hands of theirs aren't soft at all," he said. "Be God no, hard as boots they are." He ran his fingers inside his grubby shirt collar.

"What did they hit you for?"

The old man laughed and took a deep swig of his pint.

"Sure I was awful stupid back then. It took me years to learn reading and writing. Not just ordinary writing, it had to be 'copper plate'. That's what they called it. And numbers too, sums and the like; God, I hated them sums."

"I thought you just did odd jobs round the place, cleaning and stuff?"

"The girls did all the cleaning, down on their knees with the buckets and the scrubbing brushes. The nuns said it was good enough for them, in their shame. Back then there was a gardener too, I used to help him a bit, but I wasn't strong enough for it. Mostly I had to answer the door or open the gates for people."

"So why all the sums and the handwriting?"

The American leaned forward intently as the old man emptied the last of his pint.

"For the books, of course."

It had taken nights of probing, but it was worth it. The American nodded to the barman for two more drinks.

"You were a bookkeeper?"

Billy smiled.

"I suppose I was, really, though they never called me that. Billy, do this, and Billy, do that, never a please or thank you."

"That must have been interesting for you, keeping the records, knowing everything that was going on."

Billy looked bemused by the comment. He took a deep draught of his new pint, and his face creased in a smile as he looked on his work in a new light.

"I never thought it was interesting," he said, "but you're right. I did know everything that was going on. It was all in my books."

The two men sat for another half hour, draining the last of the creamy stout. Billy felt proud of himself, proud of his fifty years of servitude. According to his new friend, it was important, even interesting. He had never, in his long life, been either of those two things. Buoyed up by the unfamiliar feelings, he didn't notice how quiet his companion had become as they headed home. It was not until they were back inside the high walls, treading their way across the soggy lawn, that the other man broke the silence.

"What kind of books did you write in, Billy, were they like schoolbooks or ledgers?"

"Well now, there was two kinds of books, you see, the writing ones and the numbers ones. In the writing ones it was all words, names and addresses and things. Proper names and convent names."

———

THE OLD MAN stopped at the bottom of the back steps to look for his key. Impatient with his fumbling, the American took the key and let them in. He held his tongue during the protracted ritual of ramming the bolts home and checking the locks, followed by the filling and boiling of the kettle. Finally, sipping distastefully at the strong tea that Billy favoured, he spoke.

"What do you mean convent names?" he asked idly.

"Did I not tell you about that before?"

Billy rubbed his knuckles back and forth across his

eyelids in a childish gesture. He was in the habit of lapsing into long silences, and though he took obvious pleasure in their conversations, he tired easily.

"No, I don't think you did, old buddy. I would have remembered," said his friend.

"All the girls had two of 'em, two names."

"Do you mean middle names? Your middle name is Mary, isn't it?"

"And many's the time I got a beating for it in school, I'm tellin' you."

The younger man's hands clenched around the chipped mug.

"I bet you did, Billy," he said evenly, "but tell me about the proper names and convent names; was it middle names you were talking about?"

"Lord no, them girls came in with one name, but in here they got a new one. And God help them if they forgot it! Then they'd get in trouble."

"And you had to keep a record of the two names?"

"Which two would that be?"

The American banged his mug on the table.

"Sorry, buddy, it slipped out of my hand. Anyway, the two sets of names, the proper names and the convent names...?"

"Yep, there was a book for it, a big leather book with gold numbers on the front, for the year."

His friend's face flushed, but the old man didn't notice.

"And what else was in there, Billy, home addresses maybe, next of kin?"

His voice was eager; Billy smiled and nodded.

"How did you know that? That's just the way it was. There was three columns, Home Address, Next of Kin and Date of Birth." He said the words in a sing-song, as though he knew nothing of their meaning. "I used to have to fill in every one of them. The sisters didn't like it if you went over the lines.

You could go down to the next line but not over into the next column. Do that and you got the ruler across your knuckles," said Billy.

As he spoke, he looked down at the knuckles in question.

"I'd love to see some of that copper-plate handwriting of yours, Billy. Where are those books these days?"

The American made the question sound casual, but the old man had drifted off, his eyes fixed on the kitchen table as though it were inlaid with precious inscriptions. A vein stood out in the American's temple, and his eyes narrowed as the silence lingered between them. He got up, stood for a moment looking down on his housemate, then walked to the sink with his half-full mug. As he washed up, Billy rose and yawned his way to the bedroom off the kitchen. His guest gripped the rim of the old Belfast sink, the knuckles showing white against his tanned skin. Now that he knew what he was looking for, his search would be easier, but extracting information from the old guy was slow, and he was in a hurry. Grabbing the flashlight from its hook by the back door, he called to mind the grid he had visualised in order to make the hunt more methodical. With all the dark spaces in the convent, it would take him several more nights to search every room and closet.

He had squared off the first floor into sections, starting with the Mother Superior's room where he slept. Apart from some dusty stacks of a religious magazine called *The Sacred Heart*, dating all the way back to the 1950s, it was to yield nothing of interest. Working his way along the top corridor, he came to a series of small bedrooms, which must once have been the quarters of the other nuns. More books were piled on cobwebbed shelves, *The Lives of the Saints*, a tattered and ancient guide to the Holy Land, a copy of *The Diary of Anne Frank* covered in a brown paper dust jacket.

This was the fourth room he had searched, and he was

covered in dust. His throat prickled with irritation, and he could feel his chest tightening. Not now, not an asthma attack now. It had been over two decades since he had seen any symptoms of the condition that had blighted his childhood. Now it seemed the Irish climate and the filthy detritus of the convent might bring on a relapse.

He pounded down the stairs, not caring whether he disturbed the old man. He would wake him up and force the information out of him. The door to Billy Butler's room was ajar. He pushed it back, and a shaft of light from the torch picked out the figure in the narrow bed. The American went in and crouched by the bed. Billy was curled on one side, facing the wall; he had taken off his clerical dress, shoes and pants. Huddled under several layers of grubby blankets, he was still wearing the once-white priest's shirt.

"I could snap you like a twig, old man." There was no change to Billy's rhythmic snoring. The American stood up, weighed the heavy flashlight in his hand, swinging it by the leather loop.

"Not yet though, buddy, not yet."

## 15

Kate liked Tony McMahon, son of their prime suspect. She could see he was devastated, but he was doing his best to keep it together. He began by stating clearly that his father could not have had anything to do with the murder. He wanted to see Hugh as soon as possible and told them he had a work colleague standing by to provide legal representation for his father. Then he provided a detailed account of his own whereabouts on the two nights of the murders. Unless he was lying, he had strong alibis that could be checked for both nights. Kate asked him about his family.

Tony had obviously adored his mother. He described Deirdre as a bubbly, vivacious woman, an affectionate mother who had given the two boys an idyllic childhood, almost in spite of their father's disposition. The house had been full of their friends, and she had worked as a music teacher mainly to ensure her sons never wanted for anything.

It wasn't difficult to come to the conclusion that Tony had little time for his father, whom he described as careful with money and stern. Hugh McMahon had urged the boys to pursue academic excellence; indeed he insisted on it. But that was the extent of his interest in his sons. As Tony put it, his only concern was that they would not "show him up" at the school where he was a teacher. It was their mother who ferried them to football matches, discos and gigs. It was she who welcomed their teenage friends with home-baked treats and a sympathetic ear, while Hugh locked himself away in his study, saying "he saw enough bloody kids at work".

"Did your parents get on?" said Kate.

"They must have on some level. Why else would they have stayed together for so long?"

"You tell me," said Kate.

"I don't know, I've never understood it. It seemed like they had absolutely nothing in common except us."

"They argued?" said Kate.

"Hell yes, when they were actually talking, that is. Sometimes they went for days, *God*, even weeks without speaking to one another. He'd sulk; he's good at that. Mam would just carry on as normal and ignore him."

"Was it always like that?"

"As long as I can remember. They must have been in love once, or why else would they have married? She'd been an air hostess you know, back when it was a really glamorous job. She travelled the world, New York, the Middle East – all over Europe. There are photos at home of her in uniform; she was so beautiful; she must have had any number of offers. She was on TV you know, a couple of years ago they did a feature on the Aer Lingus seventieth anniversary, and Mum and some of her work pals from way back were in it. She really sparkled that night; you could see what she must have been like back then, so vibrant and alive."

Tony McMahon's voice cracked. Kate gave him a moment.

"I can totally see what Dad saw in her. I've just never

understood what she saw in him. I asked Mam once, not that long ago, why she put up with him."

"And..."

"She wouldn't give me a straight answer. First she kind of defended him; I think it was out of loyalty. She made excuses for him, *he wasn't happy at work, he was always being passed over for promotion*. I said that was no reason to take it out on her, or us. She said lots of women had husbands who rolled home drunk every night and beat the crap out of them. Dad was never like that, so she could count herself lucky."

"Was that all she said?" said Kate.

He paused, looking almost embarrassed.

"There was more, wasn't there, Tony?"

"I asked her why she didn't leave him now that Kieran and me were off her hands. We're both working; we would have helped her to go. I even suggested that she come and stay with me, here in Dublin, until she found her feet."

"Go on..."

Tony closed his eyes.

"She said...I'm far too old to start again. This is it for me, *comfortable misery*. What kind of life is that?" He bowed his head and covered his face with his hands. "And now that's all she'll ever have; she's gone, without ever having escaped him."

"I'm going to ask you again, Tony, do you know of any instance when your father was violent or threatening towards your mother?"

He raised stricken eyes to hers, but his answer was firm.

"Never, he doesn't have it in him. He's a miserable son of a bitch, but he's weak and ineffectual. That's why he never made principal until the last few years when there was no one else."

Kate suspended the interview on the pretext of getting

coffees. Tony McMahon asked again to see his father; she nodded.

"Soon, Mr McMahon, very soon."

In the Ops Room the Murder Squad detectives were returning from their enquiries, logging reports, exchanging anecdotes quietly as they waited to report to DCI Corcoran at five o'clock sharp. A new pinboard had been set up next to the Irene Connolly one, and a civilian clerk was using thumbtacks to pin up the crime scene pictures from the McMahon killing. Consciously or not, the woman was arranging the photos from the second murder in a sequence that exactly mirrored the first.

Kate had been methodical, taking photos at the scenes from all possible angles, in particular the heads and hands of the victims. Now, side by side, the women's bloodied remains exhibited an eerie sameness. As the second board filled up, the detectives began to drift over to have a look. The resemblance did not go unnoticed, and they began discussing the possibility of a prolific murderer, or even a serial killer on the loose, on their patch. Ireland had never had a confirmed serial killer. One investigation in the mid-nineties, into the disappearance of six young women in the Leinster area, had found nothing. No bodies were found, and while no one doubted the women had been abducted and murdered, only a couple of detectives, nearing retirement, kept up the search. As the years passed, the media clamour died down, and only the families marked the anniversaries of their loss. Many people, among them senior police officers, believed the killer was behind bars, put away for an attempted abduction, but, without bodies, there was nothing to connect him to the missing women.

Now, the prospect of a serial killer on the loose filled the detectives with a heady mixture of dread and anticipation. Kate could feel a ripple of excitement in the room, and she turned away, slightly sickened. She found Jim Corcoran in his office.

"Well, what did you get from the son?" he asked.

She could tell that his second interview with McMahon Senior had not gone well.

"Nothing we didn't suspect already," she said. "They were not a happy couple, not for years. But Tony maintains the father was never violent; in fact, the victim herself told him as much only recently. She more or less told Tony she was lucky to have him, a husband who didn't beat his wife."

"How did that come out?"

"Tony asked his mother why she didn't leave him. She admitted she wasn't happy, but she considered herself to be lucky compared to other women whose husbands rolled home drunk and beat them up. Lucky, how weird is that?"

"To you it is, but we're talking about a generation of women who grew up in a different Ireland. I know my mother would have been of the same view, every second kid on our street had a drunk for a dad, and battered wives suffered in silence, mostly," said Jim.

Kate was surprised by the confidence; her boss rarely mentioned his childhood; then again, neither did she. She only knew he grew up in a working-class area of Dublin.

"Just because he didn't hit her all along doesn't mean he couldn't have snapped and run amok," said Corcoran.

"I know that; it's not impossible, just a bit unlikely, don't you think?"

"Just let me clutch at this particular straw for a little longer, will you, Hamilton? By the way, did you check out McMahon's alibi yet?"

"I'll do it now, before the meeting, and the son's while I'm at it. Shall we let Tony in to see his father?" she said.

"Might as well, the whiney little shit's not saying any more 'til he's seen his legal representative," said the DCI.

"At this stage they're still just the bereaved family, sir. We should be treating them with kid gloves, or they'll lodge an official complaint. Tony might not like his father, but he won't stand for much more from us. Blood is still thicker…"

"Hugh McMahon is a viable suspect until such time as his alibi is set in concrete," said Corcoran. "We've done nothing but our duty, based on the evidence, not least the newspapers we found in his car."

"The police ombudsman might not see it that way," said Kate and left the DI to his bad humour. As she set about establishing an alibi she knew instinctively would eliminate their one and only suspect, she hoped the rest of the squad had found something that would open a new line of enquiry. While she was on the phone, Corcoran put his head round the door.

"I'll take Junior downstairs now. Anything I need to look out for?"

Like all good police officers, Jim was an expert at recognising deception. Kate had studied the science of body language, interview methods and observation techniques with the FBI. She knew her boss's instincts, honed over many years in the job, were rarely wrong. Still, he respected her judgement and academic know-how. It was one of the things that cemented their partnership.

"Make a note of anything awkward, out of place, any odd expression or reaction between the two. Pay particular attention to Hugh; if he's guilty, he'll be ashamed to face his son."

"Right-oh. I'll see you next door in an hour or so. Maybe the foot soldiers have turned up something for us."

"I bloody hope so," said Kate, tapping out the Wexford prefix on her phone.

It took almost the entire hour to confirm McMahon's alibi. His golf partners could vouch for his movements until about 4 am, and the hotel staff were insistent that he had not left the premises. After a spate of robberies in the area, the hotel had taken on a security firm to patrol the grounds and car park. A record was kept of all cars in and out of the grounds, twenty-four hours a day. Hugh McMahon's Volvo had not been moved that night. Moreover, the night porter was adamant McMahon had not left his room between 4 am and 9.45 am when he was woken by the manager with news of his wife's murder.

As alibis go, it wasn't watertight, but it would be damned hard to disprove. Before finishing with the hotel manager, Kate had one final question. Did they have CCTV? The answer was yes, and he promised to send on the video files from the day of McMahon's arrival to his hasty departure that morning. She sat and stared at her notes. Theoretically at least, a determined and organised killer could have evaded the CCTV cameras, the night porter and the security patrols in the car park. There was even the possibility that the staff were lying. Any one of the duty team that night could have slipped off to the kitchen for a break, or found a quiet spot for a nap, leaving time for McMahon to leave unobserved.

Was it possible, Kate asked herself, for McMahon to have crept from the hotel sometime after 4 am, acquired transport (he would have to, his car never left the car park), driven or been chauffeured almost a hundred miles to Kildare, committed the brutal murder of his wife, returned to Wexford and re-entered the hotel, unnoticed, all of this in little more than five hours, with the added complication of a retired Garda sharing his twin room? Depending on the pathologist's ruling on time of death, McMahon's alibi was not absolutely watertight. Kate would have to tell Jim Corcoran that his prime suspect was not entirely in the clear, but that, on the balance of probability, he couldn't have done it. Perhaps the CCTV footage would help, but she knew that few systems cover every exit in a building, least of all the standard installations used in the private sector. Finally, she called the Detective Unit in Wexford and enlisted their help in checking out local taxi and car hire firms to see if Hugh had taken a cab or hired a car to drive himself to Celbridge. Kate promised to email a photo of the suspect to Wexford. Grabbing her camera, she made her way to the interview room. It was five minutes until Corcoran's team meeting, and she had little time for the niceties as she interrupted a quiet but seemingly intense exchange between the McMahons.

"I'm just going to get a headshot of each of you," she said. "It will help our enquiries and speed up the process of eliminating you from the investigation."

She was in no mood for resistance. Hugh looked terrible, as if he'd aged ten years in the couple of hours since his arrival at HQ. His son was still clearly distraught, yet Kate had no sense that the tragedy had brought them closer. This was a father and son bound by blood, divided by dislike.

"Is this absolutely necessary?" said Tony.

"It's just a routine procedure, sir," said Kate. "Now if you don't mind, I'll get a picture of your father first."

"When are you going to release my client...I mean my father?" said Tony, flushing at the error.

"You are free to go at any time," said Kate, taking three or four shots in quick succession, "but if you can stay put for a short while, I expect DCI Corcoran would like to see you both before you leave. Can I send in some tea or coffee, perhaps a sandwich?" she said on her way out.

"That won't be necessary. It's six o'clock now, and we'll be out of here shortly," said Tony.

"Just some cold water, please," said his father.

"Of course," said Kate.

The murmur of voices from the Ops Room signalled the start of the briefing. Unusually, Corcoran was late. Kate used the time to upload the McMahon photos onto her PC and email them to Wexford. At seven minutes past six, Corcoran strode in, and the noise died down. On the way to the top of the room, he paused by her desk.

"Well, how's McMahon's alibi?"

"Fairly solid, almost completely watertight," she said.

"Don't waste any more time on it tonight; he's probably not our man," said her boss.

Kate's eyes widened. *What could have happened in the last hour to take McMahon out of the frame?*

"There's been another killing," he said quietly, then moved quickly to the top of the room, with Kate remaining at her desk, her thoughts reeling from his words.

"Right, all of you," said Corcoran, "I'm going to keep this very brief. If you've turned up something significant, speak up now."

He paused for a few seconds, but no one seized the opportunity. Most of the detectives avoided his gaze.

"OK then, I'll expect full reports of your day in my inbox first thing," said Jim, eliciting a few groans of protest. "In the meantime I suggest you ring your wives, husbands, mothers, significant others...because they're not going to see much of you for the foreseeable. There's been another murder."

If Corcoran had pulled the pin and lobbed a grenade into the room, he wouldn't have caused a bigger commotion. As an excited babble broke out, he held a hand up for quiet and raised his voice a notch.

"It's another female victim, believed to be around the same age. That's three women in five days, three separate crime scenes. We can't be sure if they're connected right now, so keep an open mind. But if it is the same killer, then there hasn't been a case like this in Ireland in living memory."

# 16

26 DECEMBER 1967

Rosie woke with a start; she was shivering. For a moment she couldn't remember where she was. A hint of watery daylight lingered at the window, but the setting sun only served to deepen the shadows in the small room. Her bed was made up with starchy white sheets and three thin blue blankets. The wool irritated her skin. She missed her own pink satin quilt. She had thrown off the scratchy covers in her sleep, and now she was chilled to the bone. Her new watch, another Christmas present, showed it was five fifteen. After the knitting session, the nun had sent the girls to their rooms to rest. They were not supposed to visit each other or talk; Bernie had whispered this to Rosie as they slowly made their way up the endless stairs. In truth, the trek had exhausted Rosie, and she had fallen asleep the instant she lay down.

She sat up carefully, trying to avert the dizziness that had been steadily worsening recently. She took a moment to get over the light-headedness, then pushed herself awkwardly to her feet. She hadn't even unpacked her case yet. Now, looking around at the bare cell, she badly wanted her own things around her. There was a wardrobe in the corner with a rail and a few wire hangers. Rosie filled it with her new clothes. They brightened up the room, so she left the cupboard door open. Her underwear and toiletries went into the bedside cabinet. She had brought only four books, knowing her mother would keep her well supplied. There wasn't a shelf, so she propped them on the windowsill. They succeeded in taking the bare look off it. At the bottom of her case was her new transistor radio, still in its box, and some spare batteries her dad had put in. She was sure it would be frowned upon by the nuns, so she left it there in the case, covered with her overcoat, then closed the lid and pushed the case under her bed.

She promised herself she would tune it in later to Radio Luxembourg. She knew that was the station the boarders at her school listened to at night in their dorms. They were well up on all the latest pop songs, even though they had no television. Rosie had never bothered with the radio before; she watched *Top of the Pops* on the BBC. The thought of curling up on the sofa to watch TV with her mum brought a lump to her throat. She was rummaging in her bedside locker for a hankie when there was a light tap, and Bernie put her head round the door, holding a finger to her lips. Without a word, she beckoned Rosie to come with her. Curious, and no longer tearful, she followed her new friend along the corridor, down some narrow stairs, along an identical landing to the last door in a long line. Inside they found Annie and two of the other girls from the lunch table. They were perched comfortably in a row along the rim of an enormous bath. It was twice the size of the bath at home, standing on four huge carved feet. The room was filled with cigarette smoke.

"Come on in; fancy a smoke?" said Annie.

"No, thanks, I don't smoke," said Rosie as the horrific

memory of her first and last cigarette popped uninvited into her head.

Bernie gestured to the closed toilet seat, and Rosie was glad to sit down, relieved she wasn't going to have to squeeze her swollen body onto the edge of the bath.

"Welcome to the Bath Club!"

The speaker was a girl called Geraldine. She drew long and hard on her cigarette, then exhaled with an exaggerated expression of pleasure.

"Or the Bath Tub!" They all giggled, including Rosie.

"More like the Pudding Club," said Bernie, setting off another round of giggles.

Soon they were chatting like old friends, and Rosie relaxed. There were no awkward questions about her pregnancy; they were just five teenagers, talking like teenagers do, about music and pop stars and the TV and the film stars they fancied.

It was to be the start of a new routine for Rosie. The nuns were distant, severe, but not unkind or cruel. There were a lot of prayers and Mass every day, but in that it was no different than her convent school. She settled in quickly. She and Bernie became so close it seemed like they had known each other for years. Over whispered afternoon huddles in one or the other of their rooms, Rosie learned that Bernie was the daughter of a schoolteacher and a shopkeeper in a busy Midlands town. Within days Rosie knew everything about her, including the identity of her baby's father, the captain of the local GAA team. Bernie's earlier boast, about running away to get married, struck Rosie as a little bit of wishful thinking. Bernie's "boyfriend" was the town heart-throb, and Bernie had admitted she was just one of several girls he fancied.

"He's gorgeous, Rosie, really handsome. I know he'll run away with me just as soon as I get out of this dump," she said.

"And what about your baby? Will you take it with you?"

"No way, we're too young for a baby. That's what Seamus says; it would really tie us down. He's very ambitious; he wants to go to college in America. Did I tell you he's a great runner? County champion at cross-country. When his Leaving Cert is over, he has a good chance of an athletics scholarship to Notre Dame," said Bernie.

"And he'll take you with him?"

"I hope so." Bernie's voice faltered. "He didn't promise or anything, but I've been writing to him, and he sent me a lovely card for Christmas."

"You were in here for Christmas?"

"Yes, my parents insisted. In our town if this got out" – she patted her bump – "there'd be a terrible scandal. My mam would be sacked from the school, and the whole town would rub it into Daddy's face every time they came in the shop."

"So how long have you been here?"

"A month now, seems like a year."

"What have they told people?"

"I'm supposed to be in England, visiting my auntie in Birmingham."

"What about school?"

"I've left. The nuns think I'm going to school in England. Mam told them it was the best way to get into nursing over there. That's what I always wanted to be, a nurse."

"You still can, can't you?" asked Rosie.

"Maybe, after me and Seamus get married. I might have to study at night or something. Mam says I'm going to England afterwards anyway. My auntie is a staff nurse in a big hospital over there, so she'll know how to go about it."

"Maybe Seamus will go with you," said Rosie.

"It's all a bit up in the air, I suppose," said Bernie. "What about you? What will you do?"

Rosie went silent. She hadn't thought about "afterwards".

She would have to bring the subject up with her parents on their next visit. Her old life seemed so different.

"I don't know, I might go back to school; they think I've got some heart condition brought on by scarlet fever. I should be doing the Inter this year, but I'll definitely fail at this rate. I haven't been in school since last June."

"Was that when you found out..." asked Bernie.

"That's when it happened, last July," said Rosie quietly, feeling her face redden. Bernie let the silence soften between them. Finally, Rosie spoke. "I was raped...by my first cousin."

It was the first time she had said the words aloud; a tear rolled slowly down her cheek. Bernie put her arms around the younger girl and rocked her gently.

"You poor little thing," she said.

## 17

Corcoran's words had sent a shock wave around the squad room. He didn't have to ask for quiet.

"Hamilton and I will attend the latest scene. Lawless, Sutton and Gardiner, you follow us; the rest of you carry on with your enquiries into the Connolly and McMahon cases. If they're linked, and there's a real possibility they are, we need to keep close track of all lines of enquiry. Ferguson in IT has set up a new dedicated database. It's named IRENE after the first victim. Enter every single piece of information you uncover into that system, no matter how trivial. That way IT will be able to cross-reference the data and pick up on any useful connections. You all know what happened in Yorkshire; it's textbook stuff; let's not make the same mistakes."

Corcoran was alluding to the case of the so-called Yorkshire Ripper, a sadistic serial killer who evaded UK police in the late seventies and early eighties. The public remembered the fear that stalked the northern English towns where he preyed on lone vulnerable women. But for police forces around the world, Yorkshire had become a byword for a mismanaged investigation. After hundreds of thousands of man-hours, over five years, during which the killer, Peter Sutcliffe, was interviewed on seven separate occasions by different divisions, he was finally arrested almost by accident. Had an efficient database been set up, even the basic computer programmes of the time would have pinpointed Sutcliffe's name as a prime suspect long before his killing spree had claimed thirteen lives, but the Yorkshire force had filled a vast room with index cards and paper, and the killer had evaded them for years. Corcoran was laying down a warning – don't screw this up, not on his watch.

In the Ops Room Corcoran stood with Richie Lawless, Joe Sutton and Rory Gardiner. Rory was the youngest detective in the squad, only twenty-eight. Kate was glad he was on board given the issues she had with Lawless and Sutton. She didn't relish working with two men she hated. Rory was intelligent, cool-headed and keen. With only six months on the squad, he lacked experience, but Kate was sure he would step up. He reminded her of herself just a few years earlier. Gardiner nodded to Kate.

"The call came in an hour ago," said Jim Corcoran. "The sergeant didn't immediately realise the significance, which is why I wasn't told it was a suspicious death until now."

"Where?" said Kate.

"Rathgar," said Jim. "It seemed at first to be some sort of freak accident. The husband found her. He called 999, and an ambulance and squad car were dispatched. It looked like the victim had fallen through a glass door and bled out on the kitchen floor," said Corcoran.

"So who says it's murder?" asked Rory Gardiner.

"The family doctor was called. He took one look at the dead woman and knew it wasn't an accident. Something about the nature of her injuries, not consistent with a fall through glass, so he called the local station. The husband apparently collapsed, so he had to be sent to hospital by ambulance. The local guards sealed the scene and called us. Harriet went straight there. I just got off the phone to her."

"Any details?" said Kate.

"Not yet. All she said is that there are striking similarities with the wound pattern," said Jim.

"How do you want us to work this?" asked Sutton.

"You and Lawless go door to door. Leave the murder scene to us. Look for CCTV within a mile radius of the house. We might get lucky. Here's the address," said Jim, handing over a slip of paper.

Kate was thinking about the murder scene; the victim had bled out on the floor. It was going to be a gruesome sight, picking over the remains of another killing. The familiar nausea welled up in her stomach. As Lawless and Sutton turned away, Jim interrupted her thoughts.

"Are you up to another scene of crime? You look bloody awful," he said quietly.

Kate felt herself blush. She wondered irritably if he would have offered any of her male colleagues a get-out.

"This will be body number three for us this week, I'm sure as hell not looking forward to it, and you look done in," said Jim.

"I'm fine, boss. I wouldn't want to miss this, especially if it's connected," said Kate. "What's Gardiner going to do?"

"I want him to shadow you; a second pair of eyes can't do any harm. Show him how to work the scene, take your shots, talk him through it. It's high time he got some hands-on."

"Thank you, sir, I really appreciate the opportunity," said Rory Gardiner.

On his way out the door, Richie Lawless couldn't resist a murmured, "Lick!" at the younger officer. Corcoran didn't hear, but Kate mouthed, "Fuck off!" at him and hoped Rory hadn't heard the jibe.

As they made their way to the car park, Kate suddenly remembered their prime suspect.

"What about Hugh McMahon and his son? They're still in the interview room."

"I let them go," said Corcoran. "They can't go back to Kildare; the Technical Bureau are still on-site. They'll go to the son's place in the Docklands. I know where they'll be."

"Did you tell them about this killing?"

"No. Hugh McMahon is still a suspect in the murder of his wife. We can't be sure this one will clear him just because he was in custody. It could be a different killer, an unrelated case; we won't know 'til we see it."

"We won't know for sure even then," said Kate. The three were en route in moments. Rory was a confident driver and, at Corcoran's instructions, had the unmarked Audi on flashing blue lights and siren.

"What did you think of McMahon Junior?" said Corcoran.

"He's not what you'd call devoted to his dad," said Kate.

"There's no love lost there. The father started whining the minute he saw Tony, but they were as awkward as hell with one another, never touched, not even a handshake or a hug."

"Is the husband a serious suspect?" asked Gardiner, steering the car through the parting procession of commuters.

"The husband is always a suspect until proven other-wise," said Corcoran.

"They didn't get on; sounds like a miserable marriage," added Kate.

"Was he violent towards the victim?" said Gardiner.

"Not as far as we can tell, no reports of a domestic at that house. We'll see if the PM shows up evidence of old injuries," said Jim.

"Did he not have an alibi, the golf trip?"

"That's his story, and he hasn't wavered from it. We can

confirm his whereabouts for most of the night of the murder, but not all of it. The group were drinking heavily," said Kate.

Corcoran interrupted them.

"He's a weasel of a man, that McMahon. But at the moment I can't see him carving up two women in three days. He doesn't strike me as the type for that kind of violence. The important thing at this point, Gardiner, is that he's given us a link between the two victims."

"What link is that?"

"They were friends, going back to their single days. They worked together in the sixties and seventies; they were air hostesses," said Kate.

"Wow, that can't be a coincidence," said the young detective excitedly.

Kate wasn't so sure; with another murder scene fast approaching, she was beginning to question every theory they had come up with so far.

"Statistically, you're right. There's no such thing as coincidence, not in murder. But this is Ireland; the truth is it's hard *not* to find a link between two people of a similar age if you look hard enough," she said.

They arrived at the scene, and Gardiner pulled the Audi in behind two squad cars and a morgue wagon parked outside a row of Edwardian red-bricks.

"Six degrees of separation," murmured Gardiner, opening the back door for Kate.

"In Ireland there's rarely more than three," she said.

Smoke drifted from the chimneys, hanging in the air around the yellow street lights. The neighbours were probably settling down to a meal and an evening in front of the TV. Few had noticed the commotion at number 242. The paths were wet from earlier showers, and soggy mounds of leaves had drifted against the garden walls. As the three officers put on their boiler suits, it was eerily quiet on the footpath outside the house. Bromleigh Park was a dead end; the road finished in a neat circle with a flower bed in the middle. As Kate pulled on her white rubber boots, she recognised Richie Lawless's car pulling into a space behind them.

"What the hell kept those two? They left before us," said Corcoran.

"Probably couldn't find it," said Kate. "We don't get a lot of call-outs around here."

"Probably couldn't find their way out of Phelan's bar," said Rory under his breath so that only Kate could hear.

She smiled, he might be green, but he wasn't stupid. He wasn't a typical cop. She had heard some of them refer to him as "Pansy" Gardiner. He didn't fit the Garda mould: hard-drinking, conservative, sexist. He was quiet, not very sociable, a little intense. The nickname might be a play on his surname, or perhaps it was a symptom of the homophobia that lurked just beneath the surface in the force. Kate didn't care what his sexual orientation was, but it occurred to her that if he was gay, he'd chosen a tough career path.

As they approached the house, Kate's mobile vibrated in her pocket.

"I'll just be a moment; don't start without me," she said.

It was her home number. She realised it must be Greg.

"Hi, sorry I haven't been in touch."

"It's OK, I know, I saw the news. There's been another killing."

"Yes. I'm at the scene now," said Kate.

"Don't hang up, honey; there's been a call from the retire-ment home where your mom lives."

Kate felt her breath catch in her throat. Her phone had been at the bottom of her bag all day, on silent, which was her habit while at work. Taking a personal call while on the job was still frowned upon, particularly by Corcoran, who would read the Riot Act to anyone whose phone sounded or even vibrated within earshot. Kate had only caught Greg's call because she'd pocketed her phone and left her bag in the car.

"What's happened?"

"She's OK, but she's had some kind of fall; they wouldn't give me any more details. The doctor wants to send her to hospital, just as a precaution."

"Oh my God, Greg, poor Mum. She hates hospitals."

"Listen, Kate, they say she's not in any danger; they just want to run a few X-rays. But they need someone to go with her, and they can't spare any staff member. Is there someone I can call?"

Corcoran, who had ignored her request to wait, came back out the front door of the house and looked pointedly at Kate. She turned her back.

"There's only me; she has no one else."

"But you're kinda tied up right now. Why don't I go with her? I've got nothing planned tonight."

Kate felt a lump in her throat. It had been five days since she'd seen her mother, the guilt was intense, and Greg's offer made it worse.

"You'd do that?" she said.

"Sure I would; it's no big deal. I'll bring a book. They just need someone to wait with her – I can handle it."

"But you've never met her," said Kate.

"From what you say, she wouldn't remember if I had! I'll just hang on in there until you get free."

"Which hospital?"

"St Columba's, I'll take a cab and meet her there."

"OK. I'll get there as soon as I can, but call me if anything happens, or if she needs me."

Kate ended the call and turned back to the victim's house. Corcoran stood on the doorstep, his face a picture of annoyance.

"Between the bloody husband, the paramedics and our

own officers, the place is a shambles; there's no way it's not contaminated. And they've had to ship the husband off in an ambulance; the doctor suspected he was having a heart attack. So we won't be able to question him for a while."

As she walked into the pool of light in the porch, Corcoran saw her face.

"What's wrong?"

She told him.

"Go now, Kate; we'll manage here. Gardiner and myself will do the scene."

"No, he's way too new; you might miss something. I want to do it. A friend of mine is going to the hospital; if they need me, they'll call."

Kate could see Jim wanted to do the right thing, but he needed her. As for her, part of her was more afraid of what she might find at St Columba's than what lay inside the house. Greg would call if she were needed; this way she would not have time to worry.

An hour later, Greg texted to say her mother was being admitted overnight for observation, but all the X-rays were clear.

> We're having a great chat, she's spilling the beans on you! No need to come to the hospital, she'll be going to sleep soon. See you back at the apartment x

Kate's reply was heartfelt.

> Thanks, you're the best.

Kate was exhausted as she parked the car in the under-ground garage of her apartment block. It was past midnight, and though her feet were heavy, her mind was still racing. She had spent all evening at the murder scene in Rathgar.

There were some similarities with the other two stabbings, but this time the victim had put up a fight, and far from being staged like the first two killings, the crime scene was messy and chaotic. Corcoran was keen to connect it to the other deaths, but Kate had her doubts. The victim, whose name was Phyllis Berry, was proving to be elusive. After hours of sifting through the house, Kate still knew little of the victim. With the husband in intensive care, unable to be questioned, it remained to be seen if there had been an intruder at all. There had been no signs of a break-in, and it was not unknown for domestic violence to break out even in a marriage of many years. There were no children to question. The couple were retired civil servants.

Kate pressed the lift button, too weary to take the stairs to her third-floor home. If the Gardai couldn't find a link with the other two victims, they would have to assume there were two sadistic killers on the loose, and not enough manpower for separate enquiries.

# 18

## 16 FEBRUARY 1968

Rosie Jackson went into labour four weeks before the due date Dr Magnier had given her, and eight weeks before the date her mother had calculated. It was a memorable day in the convent, not because of poor Rosie's labour, but because the Archbishop was paying a visit. For weeks the normally dull routine had been disrupted by feverish preparations. Several new girls had come since Rosie's arrival, and the rooms were all occupied. No one was excused cleaning duties, though Rosie and the others in advanced stages of pregnancy were given only light dusting. The nuns and the girls had scrubbed the entire building, furniture had been moved, statues and pictures taken down and cleaned, tablecloths and curtains washed. Poor Billy Butler and the gardener had been ordered to cut back every shrub and blade of grass in the garden to within an inch of its life. Every second of the visit had been rehearsed. The girls were told never to meet his gaze but to look at their polished shoes at all times, heads bowed, backs straight.

The day of the great event dawned grey and cold. At early

Mass even the nuns seemed skittish and distracted. At precisely twelve forty-five, a quarter of an hour before the expected arrival, fourteen girls lined up seven on either side of the front hall. They wore their dark blue flannel dresses, covered with starched white smocks that they had sewn themselves. Their sleeves were rolled up to their elbows and fixed with white elasticated cuffs, also handsewn, with a matching white band keeping any unruly hair out of sight. Over and over they practised the genuflection with Sister Hyacinth; each girl had to sink to her knees as the Archbishop passed, their hands joined in prayer. On each side of the hall seven girls were to sink like toppling dominoes as he swept along the shiny tiles. Rosie found it gruelling. After three attempts, she felt faint and was allowed to sit on the stairs until the tolling of a handbell by Billy Butler announced the arrival of the Archbishop.

The front door had been open for several minutes, and the girls shivered as much from the cold February air swirling round their bare ankles as from excitement. The Mother Superior and some of the older nuns gathered on the front step. Billy ran up the drive behind the huge black car and positioned himself, breathless and head bowed, to open the rear passenger door. First to emerge was a young priest in full cassock and tricorn hat; then he helped the Archbishop out.

Mother Superior was down the steps in an instant, and by the time the sour-faced old man looked up, she was on her knees in the gravel. He dropped his left hand, and the nun kissed the ring of office that gleamed on his bony finger. Then he began a slow ascent towards the front door, allowing the waiting nuns to kneel in turn before him and kiss the ring that signified his position in the Roman Catholic hierarchy. Finally he reached the hall and the waiting girls. The well-oiled machine swung into action, and all went well as he paced unsmiling between the two lines of bowed heads. Sister Hyacinth, holding her breath as she watched from the shadows, was on the point of relaxing, relieved that it had all passed without incident, when the Archbishop stopped abruptly alongside the last two members of the guard of honour. Rosie and Bernie had been placed last in line in the hope that their prominent stomachs would be less noticeable in the darker part of the hall. As she sank to her knees, Rosie felt a strange popping sensation and was stunned to feel a torrent of liquid gush between her legs and spread in a pool across the floor. It was this that had stopped the Archbishop in his tracks. Now he stood stock-still, looking with some alarm at his polished Italian leather slip-ons, in serious danger of getting wet.

Sister Hyacinth stepped from the shadows, bowed to the Archbishop and leaned down to help Rosie to her feet. Her face had gone deathly pale, and the act of standing up sent more fluid out from beneath her dress. The Archbishop stepped back abruptly, bumping into the Mother Superior bringing up the rear. Some of the girls began to giggle. Finally, with Bernie on one side and Sister Hyacinth on the other, Rosie was led away. The Archbishop, his mouth a thin line, stepped gingerly over the wet patch and allowed himself to be led into the parlour. The girls filed away as shocked nuns gathered around the Archbishop, anxious to soothe his ruffled feathers with a lavish lunch.

Rosie's labour was hard. Even Sister Hyacinth, who had delivered more than a hundred babies, was shocked at the fourteen-year-old's agony. Going against convent policy, she telephoned Dr Magnier after a couple of hours.

"I'm worried, Doctor, she's just a little girl, and the pain seems to be very severe. Something's not right."

"Have you checked for dilation?" asked the doctor.

"It's barely started at the moment, but the pains are only three minutes apart, and there's something else..."

"Yes, Sister?"

"I thought I got two heartbeats..."

"I think that's very unlikely, Sister. I have examined the girl several times," said Magnier.

The nun was not going to be fobbed off. Like all good midwives, she had an almost psychic ability to judge the progress of a labour, and this one had made her very anxious.

"I have a strong feeling we'll have to transfer her to Holles Street. If you wish, I'll call an ambulance and take her there myself."

"That won't be necessary, Sister. I'll be with you in fifteen minutes."

By the time Magnier arrived, the Archbishop had departed St Mary's, only slightly mollified by the fawning of the Holy Sisters and the superb lunch. Magnier hurried along the dark corridors. Childbirth was both rare and risky in a fourteen-year-old, and the dangers were multiplied many times if Sister Hyacinth was correct and it was to be twins. He should have spotted it sooner, and he remembered now the protests of the girl's mother at their first meeting. The uterus had been bigger than expected on examination, making him assume she was lying to her parents about the rape. Rosie Jackson was a very pretty girl. He had thought that a teenage romance had gone too far, as was often the case, in his experience.

In the infirmary Rosie had lost all track of time. She was in a waking nightmare far worse than the rape. Nothing had prepared her for the pain, not the whispers of the other girls, nor the stern warnings of the nuns. Her whole body was consumed by a tightening band of steel around her stomach. With each contraction she gave herself up to death, only to feel the agony ebb away a minute later, to be replaced by dread as the next wave approached. She was too exhausted to scream.

Magnier was not a man to panic, but the signs weren't good. Rosie's blood pressure was dangerously high, she was feverish and weak, and her heart rate was through the roof. He put his stethoscope to her abdomen, moving it inch by inch until he got the faint thrup of a foetal heartbeat. He moved on until he picked up a second weaker one. *Christ! The nun was right; this is going to be tricky.*

"Call Holles Street now, Sister. Get an ambulance here immediately. They're to prep the theatre; we'll need an anaesthetist and a paediatrician on standby and two incubators. This girl cannot deliver these babies herself. She needs a C-section."

It took the ambulance only minutes to arrive, but Magnier was already considering doing a C-section there in the convent, with the very real risk of losing all three lives. Finally Rosie was lifted into a creaky old wheelchair by the ambulance crew, then wheeled at speed along the corridors and carried down the front steps and into the ambulance. Sister Hyacinth and Dr Magnier climbed in, and it set off under flashing lights. At the upstairs windows Bernie and the other girls looked on, thrilled and horrified by the drama. Soon they were ushered away by the nuns, all of them, girls and women, shaken by the events of the last couple of hours.

In Blackrock, Marina Jackson took the call from the convent on her own; Sean was out of town on business. She knew immediately things were not right. It was too early; Rosie was not due for another two months. Marina put down the phone shakily. *How can I contact Sean? I have no idea exactly where he is.* Calling a local taxi firm, she grabbed her coat and bag and set off for the hospital where, only a few years before, her precious daughter had been born. She would not think about the baby, she told herself; she had to keep strong and stay focused on her own child. Rosie would need her now more than any day in her life. As for the baby, well, he or she would soon be no concern of theirs. Marina Jackson prayed and prayed that the course of action she and Sean had taken to protect their little girl would not come back to haunt all three of them.

# 19

JANUARY 2010

T he American and Billy Butler had been sharing the dusty confines of the convent for two weeks when he began to be afraid of his guest. It was nothing he could put his finger on. He simply felt a terrible dread. It gripped him every time the American returned from his excursions. After their first few nights, when Billy had regaled him with the minutiae of his long stewardship at St Mary's, the visitor seemed to lose interest in the stories. Larkin stopped going to the pub. Billy learned to fear the sound of the other man's key in the front door. Sometimes he prayed that the Yank would not come back at all.

Billy had long believed that all of the nuns he had ever known, the kind and the cruel ones, were up in Heaven, watching his every move. Alone in his little room behind the kitchen, he asked them to look down on him and send the Yank away. He rarely spoke to Billy now; he never ate or drank in the kitchen, but spent all his time scouring the disused rooms upstairs. When there was no sign of the nuns answering his prayers, Billy decided to ask his only real acquaintance in the world, the pub barman, for advice.

"Bloody Yanks, they're always the same; give them an inch and they'll take a mile," said the barman. "Just show him the door, Billy, give him his marching orders, pronto."

Then he laughed, as if it was the silliest problem in the world, which was no help at all. However, the next morning, after a fitful night, listening as the American tore apart what was left of the fittings and furnishings upstairs, Billy was presented with a solution. The Yank had gone out before Billy woke up, and the old man was relaxing with a cup of tea when someone knocked loudly at the front door. By the time he had made his way up from the cellar kitchen, the knocker had been hammered twice more. Billy opened the door a couple of inches and peered out.

"Mr Butler, I take it?" A young man stood on the doorstep, in a neat suit and a very white shirt. He had a black clipboard and wore sunglasses even though it was the middle of winter.

"Yes."

"Jonathan Byrne, of O'Mahony Reid Property Agents." The stranger held out his hand. Billy opened the door a few inches more but did not shake hands.

"We're handling the sale of the property. I just wanted to take a few measurements inside."

Byrne stepped closer to the door, then stopped, his eyes fixed on the old man's puzzled expression. He looked down to consult his clipboard.

"Have the convent's owners not been in touch, Mr Butler?"

"How do you mean?"

"The Daughters of the Cross in Dijon." He sighed. "Did the nuns not write or telephone you?"

"No, sir, I haven't had word from the nuns since they left two years ago."

Jonathan Byrne took off his sunglasses.

"Would you mind if I came in, Mr Butler, just for a little chat?"

Billy pondered the suggestion, then eased back the creaky door and led the way silently down to the kitchen.

"Well, this is some place, isn't it?"

The young man smiled reassuringly and plonked himself down on a kitchen chair. Checking his watch again, he calculated he had about an hour before his next appointment, hardly time enough to get the old boy's co-operation *and* survey the premises. *I'll kick up blue murder back at the branch. No one warned me that the caretaker is nearly as decrepit as the convent itself.*

"So how long have you been here, Mr Butler?"

"More than fifty years now."

"Well, Mr Butler, the order in France have decided to sell this place; it goes on the market in the next few days."

Billy heard the words but couldn't quite grasp what the whole thing meant. "Will there be new nuns coming?" he asked.

"No, I don't think so. In fact, we're marketing the place as a development site."

Billy looked blankly at the stranger. Byrne spoke again more slowly.

"This is what's going to happen, Mr Butler. After I've had a look around today, some more people will come by to look at the site and the building. In a few weeks' time there will be an auction, that is a public sale. Someone is going to buy this place from the nuns, and for a great deal of money."

Finally knowledge dawned in Billy's watery eyes, and he said the words Byrne had been expecting since he'd first knocked on the door.

"What about me?"

"Well, I have had no specific instructions regarding yourself, Mr Butler, but I will find out exactly what the vendors, that is the present owners, have in mind for you."

Jonathan knew very well that Billy Butler didn't figure largely in the calculations of the Daughters of the Cross. His only instructions had been to give the caretaker notice to quit, but he was a decent sort. He hadn't clocked up 465 points in his Leaving Cert and a Distinction in Auctioneering to turn addled old men out of their homes. He was sure the nuns would come to some arrangement for Billy if his firm put enough pressure on them. *The order stands to make a great deal of money on the sale; it is the least they can do for the poor man.* Having been to a strict Catholic school, Jonathan had little time for the clergy.

"And the American, what about him?" said Billy.

The estate agent consulted his clipboard.

"I'm sorry, who do you mean?"

Billy didn't know where to begin, so he stood up.

"You'd better come upstairs, mister; that's where he does be."

Jonathan followed the man up the mahogany staircase, beginning to regret taking pity on Billy Butler, who seemed a little touched in the head. What if he turned out to be a nutjob, intent on luring visitors to a gory fate in the creepy old house? Smiling to himself, he decided the frail caretaker would be no match for him. After all, wasn't he a fully paid-up member of the city's smartest gym?

The rooms of St Mary's Convent told a terrible story. As they went through door after door, the extent of the damage became evident. Billy had not ventured upstairs for days; the thunderous noises from above had frightened him. The American had been busy; no corner of the vast building was untouched. Wardrobes and cupboards had been torn from the walls, furniture had been upturned, and much of it lay splintered on the floor.

"What in God's name has been going on up here?" Byrne asked, relieved that the place was to be sold for development, not refurbishment. *It would take very deep pockets to fix this mess up.*

"It's the American who did this, it wasn't me. Sure haven't I been looking after the place all this time. This is his work, I'm tellin' you," said Billy Butler, his eyes watering from a combination of dust and dismay.

"This is the man who's been staying with you?" said Jonathan.

"'Twas him alright." Butler looked over his shoulder and continued, "I thought it would be just for a small while, but he's been here for weeks now, and I don't know what to say to, to...make him go away again."

The two were on the top floor. The rooms were small and cramped up here, and now that most of their contents had been ransacked, there was barely space to walk among the debris. Jonathan suddenly wanted to get out. Whoever had trashed the convent was clearly very strong and extremely pissed off. He really didn't want to come face to face with the mysterious American who struck such fear into the caretaker.

"I'll tell you what, Mr Butler, I have to head off now, but I'll come back another day to take the measurements."

Billy followed the younger man back along the corridors to the big front door, a little sorry to see him go. It had been a relief to tell someone other than the barman about the American. Perhaps this smart young fella could make him go.

"I'll send a letter to your visitor explaining about the auction and telling him he has to vacate the premises. It's probably best if you stay here for the moment until I find out what arrangements the nuns have in mind for yourself, Mr Butler."

"Can you make him go away...back where he came from?"

"You leave it to me, Mr Butler. I'll see what I can do, I promise."

The sight of the frail figure touched the estate agent. He waved as he went down the front steps two at a time, the forlorn man in the doorway provoking a stab of guilt as he hurried to the big double gates. He would not abandon Billy Butler.

# 20

Jonathan Byrne was not having much luck with the nuns in France, so he contacted their solicitors. After several calls, he finally found himself in conversation with the senior partner. Thomas Prendergast, of Hughes Prendergast and Fahey, professed ignorance of Billy Butler's predicament, only conceding after persistent probing that yes, he had heard there was a watchman, but insisting that he had no idea Butler was "live-in" help. Something about the lawyer's condescending voice irritated Jonathan, and he found himself more and more determined to champion the cause of Billy Butler.

"He's lived there for fifty years, and he has no intention of moving without some provision being made for him."

Prendergast was not biting.

"He has no rights in this matter; he's not even a sitting tenant since he has paid no rent."

Jonathan had a flash of inspiration.

"It's my understanding that any rent due was deducted at source by his employers, from his wages."

There was a long silence at the other end of the line. Jonathan hoped he wouldn't be caught out in a lie.

"For the life of me, Mr Byrne, I don't understand why it falls to you to put this man's case. He's not a relative, is he?"

"Of course not, Mr Prendergast. It falls to me only because this very morning I managed to talk him out of seeking legal advice in this matter. I said I'd arrange something for him, without the need for a court case. Your clients are anxious for a speedy sale, is that not so, Mr Prendergast?"

It was a gamble; as soon as he had said the words, Jonathan realised that the lawyer might actually benefit financially from a long drawn-out legal wrangle. Prendergast would be "on the clock".

"I will have to consult the Sisters of course." Prendergast paused. Jonathan's grip tightened on the receiver.

"It may be possible to come to an 'arrangement' for Mr Butler. May I be frank, Jonathan?"

It was the first time the lawyer had used his Christian name, and Byrne allowed himself a smile.

"Please be as frank as you wish, Tom."

"What's it going to take to get rid of him?"

"Well...I will have to talk to Mr Butler, and he may have engaged a legal team by now, Tom, but I suspect that he would be happy with somewhere decent to live...some sort of sheltered accommodation perhaps, here in the city, and of course a pension in line with the wages he gets now."

"You don't want much, do you, son?"

Prendergast's tone was clipped and cold. The mask had slipped.

"It's not me, Tom, it's the old boy himself; he sees it as his due after fifty years of loyal service."

Jonathan smiled; he had almost begun to believe in the feisty character he had created.

"I'll make the call to France now, Byrne, talk to you later today."

The line went dead.

"So it's Byrne again, is it, Tom – just when we were becoming so close!" Jonathan said into the purring receiver. He leaned back in his swivel chair, brought his shiny leather slip-ons to rest on the desk, and savoured the moment. It wasn't a daily or even weekly thing that he got the better of a lawyer, and rarely for a good cause. His satisfaction was short-lived. *Billy is one thing, but what am I going to do about the scary Yank?* He began to draft a letter. *This is going to be tricky.*

When the letter Jonathan Byrne composed so carefully arrived at St Mary's, for once the American was in. The postman rang the bell at the gate, and Billy Butler went down to meet him. They were old acquaintances, going back to the days when dozens of letters arrived weekly for the residents.

"This one's not for you, Billy," said the postman. "You have a visitor, do you?"

The old man shrank back from the envelope.

"Oh, I do, I do alright. He's the Yank that's been stayin' here for the last while," said Billy.

"Right so, will you see that he gets it? I don't want to trek all the way up to the door."

The postman pushed the letter through the bars of the padlocked gate. After a brief hesitation, Billy took it from him, turned on his heel and, without another word, set off, the envelope held by a corner. Billy was right to be nervous. The American read it quickly and flung it on the table.

"Did you tell them I was here?"

He didn't shout, but his low tone was even more alarming.

"Tell who?" the old man whispered.

"These property agents, some sort of Realtors, I guess. Did you speak to someone about me?"

Billy couldn't meet the younger man's eyes. He bit his dry

lips and clasped and unclasped his hands on the table, careful not to touch the open letter that had caused all the trouble.

"Some man called here. I don't remember his name."

"What did you tell him?"

"Nothing, I didn't tell him nothing."

The American walked slowly around the table and leaned in close.

"You told him my name."

All his life Billy had been warned about lying, how his tongue would turn black, how God would be listening, how his eyes would betray the darkness in his immortal soul. When the sisters told him that the truth would set him free, he could not picture freedom, because he had never known it. He imagined it was a bit like Heaven, without all the God stuff.

"He asked a lot of questions. I only told him the truth."

His voice quivered. Thomas Larkin walked behind his chair, too close. Billy didn't see the blow coming. As the cast-iron frying pan smashed into his skull, he was still looking anxiously at the letter. The blood that spurted from his mouth and nose, as his face hit the old pine table, showered a fine spray over it. Billy did not feel the second and third blows, the ones that so shattered his thin skull that it would take four hours for the Scene of Crime officer to extract every fragment of bone and flesh from the pine surface. He heard nothing of the American's departure from St Mary's, his suitcase made heavier by the addition of several bound ledgers and a cassock.

———

BARELY AN HOUR later Jonathan Byrne was in a buoyant mood when he climbed the convent steps. He had punched the air in celebration when the pompous lawyer Prendergast phoned. Good news, Billy Butler would be re-housed; arrangements were being put in place for him to be taken in by a religious order in the city. He would have board and lodgings for the rest of his life, and his usual pay, in return for a little handyman work. As soon as his early appointments were over that Friday, Jonathan headed for St Mary's. It was almost noon, and once he had delivered the good news, he promised himself a nice lunch in Kiely's. When he got no answer at the front door, Jonathan made his way around the back to the basement. He peered in at the sash window just as the watery noon sunshine streamed into the room. What he saw there made him fall back on the steps in horror.

It was several minutes before he stopped retching long enough to get out his mobile and dial 999. He asked for the police and an ambulance, but he knew in his heart that there was no helping Billy now. His fifty years at St Mary's had come to a bloody end. Shakily, Jonathan made his way back around the old building towards the gates, fishing in his briefcase for the spare keys that the lawyer Prendergast had sent to him. As the wail of sirens began to close in on the leafy street, he worked his way with clammy hands through the bunch, his head filled with the scene of bloodletting on the kitchen table just fifty yards from where he stood.

# 21

J im Corcoran screeched the unmarked car around yet another corner, scattering the city traffic before him.

"The press will have a field day with this," he said. "Four murders in a week – another opportunity to sling mud at us."

It was unprecedented; not even the Troubles had thrown that much at the Murder Squad, and with nowhere near enough manpower to cope.

"Who's the victim?" asked Kate.

"Some caretaker in a convent in Donnybrook. He's had his head bashed in."

"Robbery gone wrong?"

"There was no sign of a break-in, according to the first guards on the scene."

"Are there nuns in this convent?"

"No, it's been empty for a couple of years, apart from the caretaker."

"Who found him?"

"The estate agent called it in; the place is up for sale."

"Must be worth a fair bit, D4 – prime real estate."

"The religious orders are rolling in it; they own half the prime sites in the country."

The two officers were heading south of the city through heavy Friday afternoon traffic. At the traffic lights newspaper vendors weaved their way through the streams of cars, holding aloft the evening paper. TWO WOMEN BUTCHERED screamed the headline.

"Shit. What did I tell you? They're taking potshots at us already...like it's our fault we're in the middle of a bloody crime wave!"

"Or a killing spree," said Kate. "I've been thinking, if we're saying the first three are connected, could this one be part of the pattern? Or is it a random thing?"

"Oh, I don't fucking know. You're the profiler – you tell me! All I know is four people are dead in six days, and the press will be gagging to make a connection. Every pensioner in the country is scared witless. Next thing is some bachelor farmer will be out with a shotgun, taking aim at the postman."

"They could be right – the papers. Maybe we are looking at a nutcase. Did we check to see if anyone went over the wall in Dundrum?"

"Of course, I rang the head shrink after the first two killings. No one dangerous absconded in the last few weeks; we would have been on alert if they had. That lot might be bloody do-gooders, but they know well enough who they've got to keep under lock and key," said Corcoran.

"What about day-release? Some of them are allowed to go outside prior to release."

"That's only supposed to be the tame ones, not the violent types."

"I'll check again anyway," said Kate.

Corcoran swung the car through the open gates of St Mary's and parked next to the Garda car in front of the steps.

An ambulance had been driven across the grass and parked at the side of the house. Seeing that most of the activity seemed to be to the rear of the building, the two detectives changed quickly and headed that way. Once again Kate felt her stomach spasm in anxiety. *How many dead bodies am I going to have to see this week?* She followed Corcoran down to the basement entrance.

At the back door a white-faced Garda stood aside to let them in. The victim was seated, his upper body slumped across the kitchen table, one side of his face crushed into the surface, his head a bloodied mess of hair, bone and flesh, some of it brain tissue. A large amount of blood had spread over the wooden surface and dripped down onto the stone flags, forming small pools. Kate sniffed the air and quickly regretted it. She covered her mouth with her hand. There was no smell of decomposition.

"Must be fairly recent, no decomp, and the blood on the tiles is not fully congealed."

"We'll have to get Harriet Stilson down here to ascertain time of death," said Corcoran, reaching down to touch the old man's neck. "Even through the gloves he's not completely cold, so we're only talking two or three hours, at a guess."

Kate had to get out; her gag reflex was kicking in.

"Has anyone been over the rest of this place?" she asked the officer stationed at the door, his back stiff with the effort of not looking at the table.

Without turning, he answered, "Yes, sir...I mean yes, Sergeant...Gerry Flood and I were first on the scene; we checked the building top to bottom; no one else is here. Gerry's outside with the ambulance and the guy who called it in."

"I'll go," said Kate, glad of the escape.

The sergeant and two paramedics were in a huddle at the back of the open doors of the ambulance. Inside, wrapped in a blanket, sat a man of about twenty-five, his sharp haircut slick with gel. He was leaning forward, his head tilted over a sick bag.

The three men in uniform turned as Kate approached. She spoke first to the sergeant, whom she knew by sight.

"Who's the guy?"

The Garda consulted his notes.

"Jonathan Byrne."

"The estate agent?" asked Kate.

"Yes, Sergeant."

"Is he OK?"

"He's in shock, but he's alright."

"Right, Gerry," said Kate, "can you secure the scene, starting with those gates; we don't want anyone wandering in for a gawp. Then see what the boss wants you to take on. I'll talk to Mr Byrne. He's not going to pass out on me, is he?" she asked the paramedic.

"Just don't ask him to stand up; he's a bit shaky. And I wouldn't get too close."

Kate climbed into the ambulance and sat facing the man. He raised his head slowly to look at her, his eyes bloodshot from retching.

"Detective Sergeant Hamilton of the Murder Squad. I need to ask you some questions, Mr Byrne."

She kept her voice brisk and didn't offer to shake hands. There was no time for sympathy. The smell of vomit in the confined space had almost set her off.

"Tell me exactly what happened from the moment you got here."

Byrne didn't answer straight away, and when he did speak, his eyes glistened.

"Jesus Christ...I think...I think it might be all my fault."

"What do you mean, Mr Byrne?"

"Poor Billy Butler...I think this might be all my fault."

Byrne broke down, tears streaming faster than he could rub them away, his nose running.

"Jonathan, listen, I'm going to give you a few minutes to compose yourself," said Kate. She climbed down from the ambulance.

"We urgently need a full statement; please do not leave the scene," she said.

He was going to have to shape up, or Corcoran would explode.

Back in the basement Corcoran was briefing the senior Technical Bureau officer, but she managed to catch his eye. He stood aside and waved the man on into the kitchen.

"Well...how's the witness?" said Jim.

"Traumatised! I don't blame him, he's only young, and this one's enough to make anyone queasy." She peered in the kitchen window.

The body was surrounded by technicians. Mercifully, they obscured her view.

"Is he a viable suspect, the estate agent?" said Jim.

"Unlikely. We'll get the techies to bag his clothes and check him for blood spatter and trace, but I don't think they'll find anything. He didn't go inside; according to Garda Flood, he saw the body through the window. But he has got something to tell us."

"What?"

"Firstly, he knows the victim; his name is Billy Butler. Secondly, he says it's all his fault," said Kate.

Now she had his full attention. Corcoran's face lit up, and he started up the basement steps.

"It's all his fault...What else did he say?"

"Nothing else. The man's a quivering wreck."

Corcoran took the steps two at a time.

"Yes, but he's *our* quivering wreck," he said. "Come on, we're only in the way here. They haven't finished in Kildare or Rathgar yet, so the techies are up against it. All leave's been cancelled, but there's still not enough of them."

Corcoran set off around the house.

"Four in a week, we haven't seen anything like it in thirty years," he said.

Byrne had moved to sit at the back of the ambulance, legs dangling. He was gulping in the cold damp air in great mouthfuls. The paramedic sat beside him.

"He's not feeling too good, Garda," she said as they approached. Corcoran stopped and turned back towards Kate and spoke quietly.

"I don't care how he's feeling. I want him in HQ *now*, for questioning. We'll get him into that car even if I have to carry him over in a piggyback."

## 22

### 16 FEBRUARY 1968

Marina Jackson was just minutes behind the ambulance getting to the National Maternity Hospital in Holles Street. One of the oldest such institutions in the world, it was housed in a rambling red-brick Georgian building in the city centre. Marina had not been there since the day she walked down the front steps, Sean's protective arm around her, and their precious new baby clasped in her arms. No one at the front desk knew of Rosie's admission, and Marina spent several frustrating minutes waiting while a porter tried to find out her daughter's whereabouts. Finally, after several calls, he had news.

"An ambulance brought her, and they've taken her straight to theatre. You won't get to see her for a while yet. Please take a seat; you look a bit pale, if you don't mind me saying, ma'am."

A terrible fear hit Marina, almost taking her breath away.

"Is there no one I can speak to?" she asked.

"Your best bet is to sit down there in the waiting area for a minute, and I'll see if I can get one of the nurses to come down to you," said the porter.

Within minutes a nurse came and took her into an ancient lift and along corridor after corridor until finally she found herself in another waiting room. The nurse hadn't been able to answer her questions. More than an hour later, when Dr Magnier opened the door, Marina was in tears. She stood up the moment she saw him.

"Doctor, thank God you've come. How is she? Is she alright?"

His face was grim.

"She's in the recovery ward at the moment, Mrs Jackson, but her condition is critical. We had to perform an emergency C-section, and she's lost a lot of blood. There's also the toxaemia. Her blood pressure was extremely high on admission, and we're waiting for test results to confirm it, but it's a very serious condition. It's a lot to battle for such a young girl. She'll move to intensive care shortly."

Marina had to sit down. She couldn't speak. The consultant sat beside her. When her eyes cleared, she could see exhaustion etched on his face, and something else she couldn't quite identify. It might have been pity.

"Is she going to be alright, Doctor?"

Magnier put a hand on her arm before he answered.

"I can't say at the moment. I don't want to give you false hope. The next few hours will tell. Please get her father here as soon as possible. I'm sorry to say your daughter is critical."

Magnier stood up to leave. Marina grabbed his sleeve in desperation.

"Can I see her?"

"Not at the moment. We need to stabilise her vitals and get her admitted to the ICU. Perhaps then."

The door had almost closed when Marina called him back.

"Doctor...what about the baby?"

Magnier came back in.

"Mrs Jackson...I think you should concentrate your thoughts, and your prayers, on your daughter. As you know, we offer an especially discreet service in cases of this nature. If Rose's condition improves, she'll move to a private room. We will preserve her privacy in this matter as per the arrangements we made with you and your husband right at the start," he said.

"Yes, but...the baby? I'd just like to know...did the baby survive?" said Marina. For a moment it almost seemed like he could not meet her gaze.

"Mrs Jackson...Marina, Rose was delivered of twins, a boy and a girl."

Marina sat down, all colour draining from her face. As the silence lengthened, Magnier went on.

"They're premature, underweight and need help with breathing, barely alive. We're doing everything we can, but the prognosis is not good."

"Twins!" she whispered.

"In cases like this, it is better for families if they do not concern themselves with the baby, or babies. Stick to that, it's my advice."

The consultant moved to leave again, but in the doorway turned back to face her again.

"Should one or both of the infants survive, and it is unlikely," he said, "they'll go to good Catholic families. I must go now, I'm due back in theatre, and I want to check in on Rose first. Get your husband here without delay."

Then he was gone. It was all Marina could do to keep from curling up in a ball and howling, but Sean had to be told, and she made herself focus on that. There was a public phone box in the foyer downstairs, and she made her way back there. The porter changed a five-pound note into coins for her, and she called her husband's office, hoping against hope that his secretary would know how to get in contact with Sean.

"Tell him Rose is very sick; he needs to come home immediately. He's to come straight to the hospital."

"Which hospital, Mrs Jackson?" asked the girl. Marina drew in a sharp breath. The months of secrecy weighed heavily.

"Tell him Dr Magnier is looking after her; he'll know where to come."

"Right so, I think I can get him in the hotel in Ennis, he had a meeting at 4 p.m., so he should still be there. Do you want him to phone you?"

"No – it's OK. I'll be with Rosie, just tell him to get here quickly."

Marina headed back upstairs. It took her a while, but finally the signs led her to the double doors leading to the Intensive Care Unit. A notice overhead read:

MEDICAL STAFF ONLY BEYOND THIS POINT.

Through the porthole there was no sign of Magnier. The ward was divided by glass partitions into individual rooms, but she couldn't see any more than the blinking lights of monitoring machines next to unidentifiable patients shrouded in covers. After minutes of agonised waiting, a nurse came out. Marina stopped her.

"Excuse me, Nurse. I'm Rose Jackson's mother; can I please see my daughter?"

The girl's face softened in concern.

"Little Rose?"

"Yes, how is she?"

"She's not too good, but the doctor will be able to tell you more. We're still assessing her condition."

"When can I see her?"

"I can't let you in myself, just hold on here a moment, and I'll get one of the doctors to come out to you."

It was ten minutes before a doctor came out.

"Did Mr Magnier speak to you?" he asked first.

"Yes."

"Rose's condition hasn't changed. We're waiting for the lab results, but it looks like toxaemia."

"What is that?"

"It's a problem with the placenta that causes severe high blood pressure in the mother. Unfortunately in your daughter's case it was not detected until she presented in labour."

"Is there anything you can do?"

"The only treatment is to deliver the baby, and we've done that. There are risks for both mother and infant, and the C-section adds its own dangers. Plus Rose is very young; it's putting a big strain on her organs."

Marina put a hand on the doctor's arm.

"Please can I see her? I just want to sit with her," she said, her voice hoarse with anguish.

"I'll see, Mrs Jackson. We've had Rose in ICU for less than an hour; she hasn't come round from the anaesthetic. Give us a while, and we'll try to let you see her. There's a family room just along the corridor; if you wait in there, one of the nurses will come for you."

With that, he went back through the doors. Wearily she went and sat in the room, where a man in his late thirties was her only companion. He was chain-smoking, blowing the smoke out the open window beside him. They didn't exchange more than a sympathetic glance. She had never felt so helpless. *If only Sean were with me, he would know what to do. He's strong; he would make them save Rosie, whatever it took.* Leaning back against the sickly green wall, Marina closed her eyes and prayed for a miracle.

# 23

FEBRUARY 2010

After a dash through the lunchtime traffic, Jonathan Byrne, less green but still clutching a sick bag, found himself in a Garda HQ interview room. Having located one of the few Technical Bureau members still in the building to process him, the two officers waited outside while Byrne's clothes were bagged and his hands and face swabbed.

Kate leaned against the wall. Corcoran paced.

"Any news from Kildare or Rathgar?" he asked.

"Nothing – they're still processing the scenes. When those are done, all the techies are scheduled to go to the convent. That place is huge – it'll take days to examine," said Kate.

Finally, the Forensics officer finished his work, and the two could tackle Byrne.

With the video recording primed, he began his complicated story. Kate asked the questions while Jim Corcoran leaned back in his chair, his manner deceptively casual. The estate agent was still shaken, but unlike many they'd faced in this room, he was more than anxious to talk. It wasn't long before Corcoran sat up.

"Did you say there were *two* men living in St Mary's?" he asked.

"Yes, that's what Billy said. I told him the place was going under the hammer and that he had to leave. He just looked confused, blank, if you know what I mean. So I kind of simplified it. I explained he would have to move out, and he said, 'And the American, what about him?' We knew nothing about another tenant, so I was a bit surprised."

"Did he give you a name?" said Kate.

"Not then, no. He insisted I take a tour of the whole place with him. I thought it best to go along with the poor man; he was just so...so bewildered really," said Jonathan.

"What do you mean? Was he drunk or just simple-minded?" asked Corcoran.

Kate winced; political correctness was not her partner's strong suit.

"I think he's a bit..." said Jonathan, "I mean he *was* a bit on the slow side. I didn't get a smell of drink off him though he did mention he liked a pint."

"Which pub?" asked Kate.

Byrne ran a hand through his hair, which had long since lost its gelled slickness.

"I don't think he said, or if he did, I can't remember. He rambled on...and on! Not a lot made sense."

"We need as much detail as you can recall, Mr Byrne; it's very important," said Kate. Byrne was clearly trying to help; she didn't want Corcoran's impatience to rattle him.

"Tell me about this tour of the convent. You say the old man was rambling; what did he say?"

"I'm trying to remember. He seemed a bit jumpy. The place was a mess; you'll see for yourself if you go upstairs. I asked him if there'd been a break-in. It looked to me like the work of vandals, but the old man said it was the American."

"He said the American ransacked the place?"

"Yes, he was clear about that."

"A name, Mr Byrne! Did he give you a name?"

Corcoran's patience had run out.

"Eventually, yeah. I told him that both of them would have to leave. He was dead keen on getting the Yank out, but he'd nowhere to go himself. I said I'd send a letter telling the man to leave. It's on my PC, Thomas something. I put a note of it on my clipboard. It's in my car. I parked outside St Mary's."

Corcoran excused himself for the benefit of the recording and left.

"Jonathan, I'm going to give you a short break now," Kate said, "while we retrieve the clipboard from your car. I'll get someone to bring you a glass of water. I'll be back in a few minutes, and we'll carry on then."

Within half an hour the car, with its contents, had been delivered to HQ. Kate returned with the clipboard in an evidence bag. Quickly probing through the polythene, Byrne found his notes.

"Larkin, that was his name, Thomas Larkin, the American."

It was after four o'clock, and the Ops Room was almost empty. She found her boss in his office, on the phone, and scribbled the name on his pad. Back at her desk, Kate googled Thomas Larkin. There were literally thousands of entries. She began to sift through the results.

"Don't bother, Kate, it's an alias," Corcoran called out from his office.

"How do you know?"

"I got onto Passport Control, or Immigration Control or whatever they call themselves these days. There is no record of anyone entering the country with that name in the last five years."

"That doesn't mean he doesn't exist; maybe he's been here longer than that. Maybe he's not even American," said Kate.

"Anything's possible. They're doing a trawl of visas for me now. In the meantime I've pulled two lads out of Celbridge to canvas the pubs in Donnybrook and Ballsbridge. If Billy Butler was a regular in one of them, someone probably saw him with the Yank; there might even be CCTV," said Corcoran.

"Let's hope so. I'm going to carry on taking Byrne's statement, is that OK?" asked Kate.

"Yes, don't forget he could still be a suspect; this whole Yank thing might be a distraction to point us away from him. See what you think, and don't let him go until you have confirmation that his clothes are clean, no blood. If he bashed Butler's head in, he couldn't avoid blood spatter. I'm heading out to the scene to see if Forensics have come up with anything. I didn't go upstairs. I want to check out the state of the place and see if this American left behind anything that could help us trace him. At the very least there'll be prints if he's been there for weeks. Find out what Byrne meant when he said it was all his fault. I don't get that, do you?"

"No," she said, "I don't either. Leave it with me; if anything significant comes up, I'll ring you."

Jonathan Byrne had regained some colour in his face by the time Kate returned to the interview room. They took up where he had left off. Byrne described his dealings with the legal firm, acting on behalf of the religious order.

"Prendergast was very reluctant to do anything for Mr Butler, but I persuaded him that Butler might sue or claim rights as a sitting tenant. That place is up for development, and no investor wants a sitting tenant. Any legal hiccup could hold up the sale of the place for months."

"Did Mr Butler say he would take legal action?"

"No. All I know is he said he'd been there for more than fifty years, and he'd nowhere else to go."

"So he was upset about the sale?"

"He was shocked. The nuns moved to France a couple of years ago, leaving him there as a kind of caretaker, and he had no clue the sale was coming up."

"What were your contacts with the nuns?"

"I'd no direct contact. I spoke to their solicitor, Prendergast. He said the sisters wanted to sell up, and Butler had to get out, simple as that. That pissed me off big time. So much for Christian charity! Tom Prendergast, their brief, he's a bit of a shit, in my view; his attitude was rotten. I persuaded him that Billy knew his rights and would take legal action unless something was sorted out for him."

"Why would you do that?"

"Billy was just so pathetic and helpless. I felt bad turfing him out just to make a sale. And I hate nuns. I went to a convent school, still have the scars!"

"Was there any response from the lawyer?"

"You bet, within days Prendergast came back to me. That's why I went to St Mary's this morning. I had great news for the old man. The nuns had caved; they'd found him a place at another convent, as a handyman, here in Dublin. He'd have a roof over his head and a small wage for the rest of his life..."

Byrne's voice faltered at that point. Kate felt a wave of sympathy for him. He might look like a used car salesman, but, from what she could see, he was a more than decent human being.

"That was a good thing you did. Not many people would have bothered," said Kate.

"I felt sorry for him. He wasn't the full shilling."

"Tell me about the other man, Thomas Larkin, the American," said Kate.

"I never saw him; all I know is what Billy told me. He said

the American had been staying there the last few weeks. I think they met in the pub. Billy seemed a bit afraid of him. He said Larkin was the one who trashed the place."

"Did he tell you anything else about this man? It's very important."

"The old boy rambled on a bit, giving me the tour. He showed me the sisters' quarters and the girls' rooms. Maybe it was some sort of boarding school. I don't know the history of the place. I think he said the Yank was searching for something. Yes, I'm sure he said that. Billy didn't know what."

"Did he say where Larkin was?"

"No, he just came and went as he pleased. Billy never knew when he was going to be in or out."

"What then?"

"I decided to write to Thomas Larkin and give him notice to vacate. I didn't want to keep having to go back there; the place sort of spooked me. And I was wary of running into the American. He'd made a right mess of those rooms upstairs. I didn't fancy being the one to tell him face-to-face to get out."

"Did you take the letter to St Mary's?"

"No, I put it in the post."

"When?"

"Yesterday."

"So it should have arrived this morning, yes?"

Byrne looked distraught. Then after a slight pause, he spoke.

"That's my point. If this crazy American got the letter this morning, maybe that set him off," he said.

"Is that what you meant by it being your fault?" asked Kate.

"Yes, what else would it be? Look, Sergeant, I'm not making accusations or anything! God, I never even laid eyes on the man. It's just...sitting here alone, I've been going over and over the whole thing. Here's what I think...if the American was mad enough to trash the place, maybe he's crazy enough to bash in poor Billy Butler's head."

"Is there anything else you can remember? Anything that Billy said? Even a small detail could help," said Kate.

"I'm racking my brains. I was there for about an hour, I'd say, tramping up and down stairs and corridors. First off he showed me round the front of the house. That part is all big rooms with wood panelling and high ceilings. He said the Yank was using one of them."

"Do you remember which one?" asked Kate.

"Right at the front of the main house, first floor, bay window. There's an old-fashioned brass bed with a red quilt. It was the only bed that was made up, as far as I can remember."

"That's good, Jonathan; this is helpful. Did you see any personal effects, a suitcase or travel bag, any clothes, anything that might belong to the American?"

"God, I can't remember. It was neat in there compared to the other rooms, but I can't recall seeing any bags or stuff."

"What else can you remember about the convent?"

"Lots of statues, and crucifixes on the walls...I remember them. Kinda gave me the creeps. There were little shrines everywhere...and burnt-out candles, you know, the little tea lights in front of each statue."

"Go on..."

"You could get lost in that place. I tell you, I wasn't looking forward to having to survey it for the auction, or conduct the viewings, for that matter. I reckon any buyer would have two options, knock it down and start from scratch, or total refurbishment and turn it into apartments; structurally it looks sound enough."

"Did you make notes as you went around?"

"No, it would take a day or two to measure the place up. I was going to come back in overalls and rubber gloves. I only

took a few pictures to show them back at the office. We were
planning a brochure."

"Where's the camera?" asked Kate eagerly.

"It's just a cheap little Polaroid. We'd normally send in a
professional to take the glossy shots."

"Do you have those pictures?"

"No, they're at the office."

"Great, we'll need to get them as soon as possible," said
Kate. "Interview suspended at 4.35. I'm going to ask you to
wait here for just a bit longer. I'll send in some tea; you look
like you could do with it. I'll talk to Detective Inspector
Corcoran now, and we'll probably let you go shortly, just as
soon as we can get those photos from your office."

She grabbed her notebook and headed for the door.

"Jonathan, please speak to no one about this," she said.
"There's a vicious killer out there, someone with no
compunction in attacking a vulnerable man. Your family and
friends, your workmates, they'll all want to know what you
know, and the press will hound you if word gets out you were
at the scene. If you have to say something, it's best to say you
alerted the police to a suspicious death, no gory details.
When we catch Billy Butler's murderer, you *will* be called to
give evidence. Nothing can interfere with the judicial process,
do you understand?"

Byrne nodded.

"I'm not just concerned about the investigation,
Jonathan," said Kate, from the doorway, "this is also about
keeping you safe from a brutal killer."

From his expression, she was satisfied Byrne wouldn't
talk.

# 24

16 FEBRUARY 1968

The flight from Shannon to Dublin took less than half an hour, but for Sean Jackson it couldn't have felt any slower. The message from his Dublin office that Rosie was in hospital had sent him into a barely controlled panic. Running from the Ennis hotel where his meeting was taking place with barely an apology to those present, he had driven at speed to Shannon Airport, where, as luck would have it, there was a scheduled flight to the capital. The drive would have taken four hours or more; this way he could make it in under two. Now, with a large brandy in hand, he sat grey-faced and alone, with only the thought of his daughter keeping him from howling out loud.

A taxi brought him from Dublin Airport to the hospital. The porter directed him to ICU. He pushed the door to enter but was stopped by a nurse, who sent him to the waiting room. Marina was there, slumped in a plastic chair, eyes closed, tear tracks on her cheeks. She jumped at the sound of the door closing, instant fear in her expression. Wordlessly they embraced, both now crying. Eventually Sean spoke.

"What happened? It's too soon, isn't it, too early for the baby to come?"

Marina managed to answer in between sobs.

"Two months early, but that's not the worst thing, Sean. Rosie's very sick; she's in a coma. They did a caesarean as soon as she got here, but she's got something really serious wrong with her. It's bad."

For a second she thought Sean was having a heart attack. His face, which had been red with crying, went almost grey. He collapsed onto a chair as if his legs could no longer hold him up. His shoulders shuddered as she sat beside him, wondering how in God's name she could tell him the rest.

"They're doing their best for her. The doctor said she's in the best place in the country. We just have to wait and pray now."

"Can we see her? Have you seen her?" he asked.

"No, they won't let us in. I'm waiting for Dr Magnier to come back. I'm so glad you're here; it's been unbearable."

The door opened, and the consultant stepped into the room. Both the Jacksons stood up suddenly. Sean swayed slightly.

"Sit down, love; you've had a terrible fright," said Marina, fear piling up on fear in her mind.

"I think you should both sit down now, Mrs Jackson," said Magnier. "I have some very bad news."

He waited until Marina was seated, her heart exploding in her ears. Magnier sat beside her and laid his hand over hers. She looked from his face to her husband's and knew before he spoke what was to come.

"I'm so sorry. Rose never recovered consciousness. The strain of the twin pregnancy had weakened her heart; her body couldn't fight the toxaemia. We tried everything, but we lost her."

The Jacksons couldn't speak. Marina sobbed on her

husband's shoulder. He stared straight ahead, his eyes glassy and unfocused. Finally, Sean spoke.

"Did you say twin pregnancy?"

"Yes, Mr Jackson, your daughter was delivered of twins, very premature."

Sean got to his feet and in a second had Magnier by the throat up against the wall.

"You missed it, didn't you? Twins, poor little Rosie carried twins, and you never detected it," he shouted.

"Sean, stop. It's not his fault. Let him go," pleaded Marina.

"It *is* his fault. Rosie's dead, and it's his fault. You missed it, you incompetent bastard! The risks must be higher with twins, much higher. She's only fourteen." Sean choked on his words. "She *was* only fourteen."

He let the doctor go then, all the fight leaving him.

"We did our best, Mr Jackson. Toxaemia is a very dangerous condition, and I assure you twin pregnancies are not always detected pre-confinement. We don't have the technology of other countries, hi-tech scanners and the like..."

The doctor's voice tailed off. Marina finally spoke.

"Can we see her?" she asked.

"Yes of course, just give us a few minutes to...prepare her," said Magnier, looking relieved to have a reason to go.

"I'll sue you and those nuns and the hospital over this," said Sean, to his departing white coat.

Marina looked wearily at her husband.

"And what good will that do? It won't bring her back," she said.

They went quiet, each wrapped in their own pain. Soon a nurse came for them. They followed her to a side room bare of medical equipment. There were pastel-flowered curtains and a simple white crucifix over the bed.

"Oh dear Jesus, she looks like she's sleeping," said Marina, reaching out to touch Rosie with a trembling hand.

Sean held back, his eyes fixed on the still form. Marina leaned over and kissed Rosie's forehead. Her skin was not yet cold, but it felt waxy and unnatural. Her tears dropped onto the pallid cheeks, and Marina fumbled a hanky from her bag and patted her daughter's face dry.

"Come on, Sean, you have to say goodbye. Please, love, this will be our last chance."

She broke down, but still Sean was frozen where he stood.

"I can't do it. I can't."

Minutes passed, and finally Sean moved to the bedside. Marina took his hand and for a moment placed his palm gently against Rosie's china-white cheek. She knelt down by the bed and murmured a prayer. Soon the nurse returned.

"Mr Magnier wants me to ask you if you wish to visit with the babies?" Both heads turned towards her, faces shocked.

"No...we don't," said Sean.

"But, love...maybe we should..." Marina's voice failed her.

"I never want to see or hear about those babies," said Sean. The Jacksons left soon afterwards, tearing themselves away from their daughter as night fell. They didn't exchange a word or a comforting touch in the taxi on the way home.

Within a year Sean Jackson had succumbed to a heart attack, his spirit broken by grief and destroyed by alcohol. Marina Jackson remained in the big Blackrock house, isolated and reclusive, unwilling to return to her family in England, where Rosie's rapist was alive and well, still unpunished. She stayed aloof from her former friends, a widow at thirty-four, living a half-life of work and little else. She took over the running of her husband's company and saw his legacy multiply in value until she was one of the richest women in Ireland.

## 25

Corcoran was still at St Mary's when Hamilton called. They agreed Kate would take Byrne to his office, access the photos the estate agent had taken at the convent, and then join the team at the crime scene. Corcoran was convinced something in the old building would lead them to the killer. With manpower in short supply, the detective inspector was supervising and occasionally joining in the fingertip search of the premises.

"There's nothing doing in Kildare," he said. "I've sent Gardiner to speak to the Rathgar victim's husband in the hospital as soon as he's allowed to by the ICU doctors. The techies have finished in Killiney and found fuck all, as far as I can tell. Four crime scenes, it's fucking chaos. We need to concentrate on this place," said Corcoran.

"I'll be with you as soon as I can; another pair of hands might help," said Kate, and went on to tell him about the estate agent's letter.

"Byrne is convinced it triggered the attack on Billy Butler; he's all guilted out over it," she said.

"They're still processing the kitchen," said Corcoran. "I'll see if they've found it. Bring the photos; they might give us something," he added, and hung up.

Forensics had given the all-clear to Jonathan Byrne within the hour, so once she'd obtained his photos of St Mary's, Kate sent him home and made her way to Donnybrook and the latest crime scene at the convent.

For the first time in years, St Mary's was full of busy people. Corcoran had called in reinforcements from the uniform ranks. Suited up like CSIs, many of them inexperienced recruits, they were tasked with carrying out a thorough search of the dozens of rooms that had lain idle for so long, and the sprawling overgrown garden. They had been instructed, with some ferocity, by the chief inspector only to *look* for possible evidence, then mark it and leave it alone. The real crime scene technicians would follow up. In the basement the most senior of these were still combing over the bloodied remainders of Billy Butler's life and death. After some hours the victim's body had been transported to the City Mortuary once Harriet Stilson, the state pathologist, had given permission. In murder cases she insisted on seeing the body in situ; only when she had done so would she countenance the removal for post-mortem examination.

"We think he used the cast-iron frying pan," Jim Corcoran told her.

"I'll take that with me, then, if you don't mind," said Harriet, her voice softened by a face mask, "so I can assess it in conjunction with my PM."

Corcoran agreed with a nod, and the senior CSI handed over the heavy pan in its plastic evidence bag. There were traces of fingerprint powder on the handle.

"Did you get anything?" asked Corcoran.

"A good set of prints from the handle, but some smudges as well. The assailant may have worn gloves and left the smudges, in which case the prints are probably the victim's.

We've got two cups that were unwashed in the sink. Two cups – maybe two DNA profiles, with any luck," said the technician.

"Put a rush on them with the lab, will you?"

"Four murders in six days, the lab's backed up, boss, but I'll ask."

"Put a bloody rocket under them; this can't wait," said Corcoran. "I want comparison DNA tests on the most likely samples from each murder. They may be connected."

Kate was en route to St Mary's to join the fingertip search when she remembered her mother, in hospital for two days and still without a visit from her only daughter. The guilt formed a knot in her gut. She turned off and headed for St Columba's. Greg had come back late the previous evening, full of reassurance about her mother's condition, but suddenly Kate *had* to see her. It wasn't visiting hours, but the nurses let her in anyway. In just a few days her mother seemed to have shrunk. Her limbs barely made a bump under the pink coverlet. She was sleeping peacefully, though Kate had no idea how because the ward was filled with noise and movement, and the curtains round the bed did nothing to keep the chaos out. Sitting gently on the edge, Kate took her mother's hand and felt relief that it was still warm. Maura Hamilton's eyes opened, and Kate thought she saw recognition there. Her mother smiled.

"Ah, love, it's you! Where've you been?" she said.

"I'm so sorry, Mum, I've been on a case. How are you?"

"Sure I'm grand, never better, love. I went for a great walk today, Paddy and myself went all along the seafront."

It had been more than a year since her father had been resurrected by her mother's failing mind. Once or twice Kate had tried to break the news that Paddy Hamilton was more than twenty years dead, and each time it had been a devastating blow. Her mother would cry over her beloved "hand-some boy". Minutes later the questions would start again.

"Where's Paddy? He should be home by now."

Kate smiled into the still-bright blue eyes, so different from her own.

"I'm glad you had a nice walk, Mum," she said, but the spark of recognition had faded, and the old woman's face registered only anxiety. She pulled her hand away from Kate and turned her head into the pillow. In a moment she was asleep again. It seemed like each time she saw her, it might be the last, and Kate had no idea what to say or do to make it meaningful, tender, right. Her phone vibrated; she knew it would be Corcoran but ignored it. She tucked the blanket around her mother and kissed her cheek.

"To the universe, Mum," she whispered against the soft dry skin, the words taking her back a long, long way.

"I love you up to the sky," was Kate's favourite saying as a four-year-old. Her parents made it into a game.

"I love you up to the stars," her mum would reply, and her dad would cap it all with, "To the universe, my girls." Eventually, as the self-conscious years arrived, Kate rarely said it. But now and then, at times of high drama, the kind that only teenagers can create, her dad would say, "To the universe, love," with a smile. More often than not it would defuse an angry scene. Now her mother was slipping away bit by bit until soon there would be no one left to say it to. Visiting was never easy; leaving was worse. Walking to the car, Kate made a conscious effort to shake off the sights and smells of the hospital and the palpable sadness that they carried.

## 26

K ate scanned the five text messages that popped up on her phone – four missed calls and a text from Corcoran.

> Merrion Hotel, ASAP. The Head Nun is in town.

At the city centre hotel Corcoran was waiting in the lobby.

"Took you long enough; did you get anything more out of the estate agent?"

"I have the photos he took of the convent, inside and out. I'll take a closer look back at HQ, but I can't see anything in them to identify the other man."

"Pass them on to some of the Tech lads; they might be able to enlarge or enhance some detail we'd miss."

"So what's the deal with the Head Nun?"

"We contacted the legal firm that's handling the sale, and they let slip she's in town. The last few nuns from St Mary's all live in France now. There's two of them over here to see to business, apparently. I rang ahead to see if I could speak to them, but they insist on having their solicitor present, which makes me think they've got something to hide."

"Maybe, or they could just be cautious. The religious orders have taken a lot of flak lately."

"Too right they have, much of it deserved."

A tall fifty-something man in an expensive overcoat and dark suit entered the lobby. After a quick glance around, he headed straight for the two detectives.

"Detective Chief Inspector Corcoran, I presume." He smiled ingratiatingly, ignoring Kate and extending his hand towards her boss.

"Shall we get down to business, Mr Prendergast?" said Corcoran, offering the briefest of handshakes. "My colleague and I are in the middle of multiple murder enquiries, and I don't have the patience for time wasting."

"My clients have a small suite at their disposal. I'll get reception to advise them of our arrival," replied the lawyer briskly.

The nuns' small suite turned out to be generous. Using a swipe entry card he'd been given by reception, Prendergast led them inside. Two sofas and a coffee table were grouped around a faux electric fireplace, and by the window there was a separate raised area clearly intended for room service dining or entertaining. A wide double door, evidently leading to the bedroom, opened, and two nuns entered. The younger was a neat woman in her forties in a navy suit and a white shirt closed to the neck. Her older companion was in full black religious habit, with a short veil that concealed all but a few strands of white hair on her forehead. She walked slowly with a limp. After formal introductions they took their seats with Prendergast on one side of the table. Corcoran and Kate sat opposite. The lawyer had discreetly managed to arrange the chairs to make the lines of engagement very clear. He was the first to speak.

"I'm sure you'll understand that Mother Marie Claire and Sister Walter Dominic are very shocked by the...events at the convent. Their main purpose here was to take care of matters relating to the sale, and this has been a very unwelcome development. As theirs is a short visit, I hope you'll be able to keep things brief."

Corcoran ignored him.

"You have our sympathies on the loss of your employee Mr Butler, but the main concern of An Garda Siochána must be the successful investigation of this brutal crime."

The younger nun winced at the words. The older one produced a tiny lace handkerchief from one of the many folds of her habit and held it to her mouth. Kate began the questioning.

"We need to find out as much as possible about Mr Butler, to help us track down his killer. Can I ask if you knew him personally?"

"Not at all, Detective, I have never been based in this country," said the younger nun. "My work has always been in the headquarters of the order, in Dijon. You're quite certain, are you, that it was a murder?"

Her accent was English and had the clipped precision of someone who lived among non-English speakers. She seemed oblivious to the tears of her companion.

"Yes, there's no doubt. Sister Walter Dominic, I take it you *did* know Billy Butler," said Corcoran.

The old nun sniffed. When she spoke, her voice belied her outward fragility.

"I knew him from a boy, poor Billy. May the Lord have mercy on his soul."

Her accent was unmistakably Irish.

"Tell me about him, Sister. He'd been at St Mary's a long time, I believe."

"Nearly as long as myself, Garda. Billy came to us straight

from school. He was from a good family, but he wasn't a great scholar. He only learned to read and write when he came to us, but he was a good worker."

"And what was the nature of his work, Sister?" asked Kate.

The Mother Superior, who had seemed to Kate to be getting increasingly uncomfortable, interrupted.

"Mr Butler was a handyman," she said.

The older nun was not to be hushed, however.

"No, no, poor Billy was useless as a handyman, too clumsy altogether. Once he learned how to read and write, he was good for nothing, only bookkeeping."

For an instant a flash of annoyance crossed the younger nun's face. Kate wondered what it was that had unsettled her. Corcoran had picked up on it too. *Could it be that there was something in the books that Billy Butler worked on that the nuns didn't want made public?*

"Can you tell us the nature of the 'work' of the order at St Mary's?"

Silence.

"It was a place of retreat, in the main," said the Mother Superior.

A mute tension spread between the five people around the table. Prendergast cleared his throat to speak, but the old nun beat him to it.

"We looked after girls who got into trouble...fallen women," she said.

The Mother Superior's mouth tightened into a thin line. Corcoran's voice hardened.

"A mother and baby home?"

Prendergast spoke up.

"No, not one of those, St Mary's was quite a different establishment from those places."

The younger nun glared at him.

"I don't see what relevance this has to your enquiry," she said, but her companion cut across her.

"We were a cut above those places, you know. Our girls had it easy compared to the laundries," said the old nun.

"Tell us, Sister, tell us about St Mary's," said Kate gently, ignoring the icy stare from the Mother Superior and the flushed look on the lawyer's face.

"Well, my dear, if you'd just get me a nice cup of tea, I'll tell you all about St Mary's. I really miss the Irish tea, you know; that French stuff is dreadful."

## 27

Rory Gardiner couldn't curb his excitement. This was his first murder case, and finally he was getting to do more than just stare at a computer screen and complete database entries for the squad. For an hour now he'd been sifting through archived staff files in a claustrophobic windowless room in Aer Lingus headquarters at Dublin Airport. He had finally located papers relating to the first two victims, Deirdre McMahon, nee Burke, and Irene Connolly, nee Quigley. Both had joined the ranks of flight crew in the mid-1960s as very young women. In the 1970s they had resigned, only months apart, as was the custom when air hostesses, as they were then known, married. Now Gardiner was searching through the work records of each woman, hoping something would emerge from the dusty, hand-written index cards and roster sheets. The clerk who had given him access to the archive popped her head round the door.

"Can I get you anything else, Detective?"

"I might need some help with some of the terms and codes on the rosters. I'm a bit baffled here..."

Quickly he showed her copies of the worksheets.

"I've worked out the routes that they worked; they were almost always on the long-haul flights, transatlantic to New York, Boston, Chicago. Often they worked together, and we know they were friends."

"Yes, you're right there. Looking at these, they certainly seemed to have worked together a lot, so they probably were good friends. Back then it was looked on as a glamorous job, with *quite the social life*, especially on those stopovers in the US."

She arched an eyebrow and smiled at Rory, and he knew exactly what she was implying. Flight crew had a reputation for partying hard, especially when air travel still had an aura of romance, even adventure, about it.

"Do you know what this means? 12 x UM? It pops up every few weeks on their flight logs, mostly New York flights but sometimes Boston as well. I can't work out what it means, sometimes the number is different, but never less than 6 or more than 16 x UM."

"Unaccompanied minors, that's the code for unaccompanied minors. We still use it today," said the clerk.

"Thank you, I never would have worked that out. Isn't it an unusual pattern though? Like every month or so a whole bunch of children travelling unaccompanied to the States?"

Gardiner felt the glimmer of an idea at the back of his mind, but couldn't quite grasp it. Meanwhile the helpful clerk had started rummaging with purpose in the archive boxes.

"Hold on, Detective, I think there's something here that might help. The company was celebrating some anniversary, and they did a TV special on us. I'm nearly sure they interviewed some of the old flight crews. I think we have a copy here somewhere; it's a VHS tape."

Half an hour later Gardiner took the stairs two at a time at Garda HQ, spurred on by an instinct that the dusty tape under his arm was important. He located a VHS player in a store cupboard piled high with fax machines, two-way radios and, of all things, an ancient metal detector.

In an empty office with a TV, he managed to hook up the VHS player and sat down to watch the tape. It was labelled:

*Aer Lingus 70 Years Sky High*

The programme was a documentary with lots of archive shots, interviews with elderly people who'd been early travellers, and retired air crew. Exactly forty-two minutes in, Rory Gardiner jumped from his chair and stabbed an urgent finger at the control buttons on the vintage VHS machine. It took him several minutes of swearing to master the pause and rewind functions, all the while his heart rate rising with the fear that he might accidentally erase the damn tape. On the third playback he was sure. There they were, the first two victims, looking younger but very recognisable, and wearing their old Aer Lingus uniforms with obvious pride. Among several nostalgic anecdotes, they told of caring for the toddlers and babies aboard flights to the US and, without a trace of embarrassment, described the joy on the faces of the waiting adoptive parents as the children were handed over. Wincing at the metallic shriek as the tape ejected from the old machine, Rory practically sprinted into the Murder Squad room.

"Where's the boss?"

No reply. Gardiner checked the ops board. Morrison Hotel was against Corcoran's name. Puzzled, Gardiner dialled Kate's number, followed by his boss's. Nothing. He couldn't wait, and twenty minutes later he was charming the hotel receptionist into disclosing the room number of the two nuns. He couldn't wait for the lift and took the stairs at a run. Corcoran opened the door to him.

"Babies," said Gardiner breathlessly, "it's about babies." Corcoran bundled the younger officer, still talking excitedly, out into the corridor.

"The first two victims took dozens, maybe hundreds of them to the States, flight after flight, for years. Overseas adoptions, probably illegal. That's the connection."

"Keep it down, Gardiner. Hamilton is interviewing two nuns in there, and guess what? They ran a mother and baby home, a private one."

"St Mary's?"

"Give that man a cigar," said Corcoran.

Inside the suite, the old nun, after the disturbance at the door that had broken the flow, was once more into her stride. It seemed like she had years of silence to break. Early on Kate asked to record the interview on her iPhone. Both the Mother Superior and the lawyer raised objections, but Sister Walter Dominic gave her permission readily. Kate took notes, but she could barely keep up, jotting only occasional words down to remind herself later.

"St Mary's was a private clinic, very discreet. The girls who came to us were respectable girls who had gotten themselves into trouble, the daughters of teachers, doctors, businessmen. Those people paid a lot of money to save their reputations. Sure if you'd a child out of holy wedlock, your whole family was disgraced, and there'd be no hope of ever marrying well. You'd nearly have to leave the country over the scandal."

Several times the younger nun attempted to halt the outpouring.

"I can't see how any of this is relevant," she said curtly. "The clinic closed many years ago; surely it can have no bearing on the death of Mr Butler."

Corcoran returned, bringing Rory Gardiner with him. After brief introductions the two men joined the gathering at the table, their presence cutting the space available for elbow room, something that clearly made the Mother Superior uncomfortable. She sat rigid, her hands clasped in her lap.

"We've come into some new information about St Mary's that means all of this may well be relevant," said Corcoran, bringing a look of alarm to her face.

Kate was keen to get the older nun talking again.

"What happened to the babies?"

"Sure they all went to good Catholic families. His Grace insisted on that."

"His Grace?"

"Archbishop John Charles McQuaid – he founded the whole scheme."

Kate had not heard of McQuaid, but clearly Corcoran had.

"Well, well, well, not surprising *he* had a hand in this," he murmured.

"Are you talking about legal adoptions?" asked Kate.

Prendergast was quick to intervene.

"Unfortunately the relevant records are no longer available, but I'm sure the sisters acted in good faith."

"You must understand," said the Mother Superior, "our knowledge of the operation of St Mary's is limited. There are few records, and only one or two of our sisters are left who ever worked there."

The old nun was not to be silenced.

"Those people had to be vetted. Their parish priest, wherever they came from, had to give them a good reference before they could get a child. They were wealthy too; that was important. They had to be so they could support the child and give it every opportunity in life. Those babies went to good homes, far better than anything their unfortunate mothers could offer."

Rory Gardiner spoke for the first time.

"They were shipped out by the planeload to the States; doesn't sound like a legal operation to me."

Kate was surprised, this was news to her, but it explained Corcoran's hardening attitude.

"I do not like your tone, Guard," said Prendergast, but Corcoran was having none of it.

"What we have here is a baby export operation on a grand scale, no doubt a profitable one, controlled and sanctioned by none other than the notorious McQuaid, a vicious man who held the government of the day in the palm of his hand. I'd hazard a guess there was little heed paid to the laws of the land. That man made his own rules."

Prendergast looked horrified, but it was the Mother Superior who took control. She stood up abruptly; such was her annoyance she briefly slipped into French.

"*Ca suffit!* Your attitude to our Church leaders is disrespectful and slanderous. This interview is over, Detective. I must ask you all to leave."

For a moment no one moved, and Corcoran and the Mother Superior exchanged a hard stare.

"This is by no means over," said the DI. "I have no doubt we will need to speak to you and your companion again. I would ask that you remain in Dublin for the next few days. May I remind you, Sister, that we are investigating the brutal killing of your employee."

He paused for effect as the Mother Superior began to help the older nun to her feet. Corcoran did not soften his attitude.

"We'll be in touch to arrange a more formal interview at Garda HQ. I suggest you bring along what records you have in your possession concerning St Mary's."

Prendergast spoke up.

"Any records would be in France, I imagine. Isn't that the case, Sister?"

"Yes, I believe so."

"Well, I suggest you get them sent over immediately," said Corcoran briskly.

"Our archives are stored digitally," said the younger nun.

"All the better," said Gardiner, handing her his card. "They can be transferred file by file directly to us at HQ, on my email address. Or you can get your people to grant me remote access."

The Mother Superior took the card.

"I still cannot see the point of any of this," she said.

"An elderly and vulnerable man, to whom you and your order owed a duty of care, has been murdered in the most violent and shocking manner," said Corcoran. "Everything about that place and its history is relevant. His whole life was bound up with St Mary's. I think it's safe to assume so was his death."

"Poor Billy Butler," said the old nun, "sure he knew all the secrets," and mopped a single tear.

## 28

Kate was quiet on the way back to HQ, the interview with the nuns had been intense, and there was something gnawing at her nerves that she knew she couldn't keep quiet anymore. At HQ she followed Corcoran into his office, closed the door and sat down, mostly to keep her legs from shaking.

"Well, what do you think?" he asked. "Do we have a real connection between the murders?"

He could barely suppress his excitement. He wanted to believe that they finally had a line of inquiry; now he wanted her to confirm it.

"There's no such thing as coincidence in murder," she said. "How many times have you told me that? St Mary's is at the centre of this whole thing, I'd lay money on it."

"Me too. So, where to from here? Those bloody nuns are not giving us much; young Gardiner should get access to the archives today or tomorrow. I don't know how much that's going to reveal? The place closed more than twenty years ago."

"There's something you should know. I should have told you sooner...I'm sorry."

"Is this about the case?"

"Yes...and no. It may be nothing, or it could be relevant," said Kate. "First, read this. It came by post, here at the station. Take a look, and you'll understand what I mean."

She handed him the letter she'd been carrying round for a couple of months. It was only one page, handwritten in blue ink.

*Dear Kate,*

*I'm not a madwoman or a crank. I loved you from the moment I held you in my arms, a tiny helpless little baby with no one but me to love you. I don't want anything from you except the chance to meet, even once. Remember this while you read this letter.*

*My name is Bernie O'Toole. I'm almost sixty now and beginning to feel my age, which might explain how I've finally found the courage to make contact. It's not that I haven't thought about you. There hasn't been a day when you weren't in my mind and my heart. Now I'm throwing caution to the winds.*

*I think you probably know this already, but here goes anyway. You were born in Holles Street Hospital on February 16, 1968, and only a few weeks later you came to St Mary's Convent in Donnybrook. It was a sort of nursing home, run by nuns, where girls like me were sent to have our babies, our 'illegitimate' babies. I looked after you and loved you until you and I left St Mary's, ironically enough, that Christmas of '68. You were sent to a guard and his wife, I believe. I expect they told you all about it. I'm sure they gave you a wonderful life, but giving you up almost broke me.*

*I went on to become a nurse in England. There were many babies to love, but never the blessing of one of my own. I was lucky to have a good man at my side until a year ago when he passed away. Losing him has made me think about a lot of things, important things that I've been putting off doing. Contacting you is top of that list.*

*You were the sweetest little baby, full of smiles and starting to make baby talk when last I saw you. I'd give the world to see you again. My address and phone number are above, or you can contact me through a Facebook Group called 'Donnybrookmarys'. It was set up last year by some of the girls who were in St Mary's, and through that group a number of amazing reunions have happened. This has given me hope that you might agree to meet with me.*

*Please get in touch.*

*With all my love,*

*Bernie O'Toole*

Corcoran said nothing for a long time. He dropped the letter onto his desk and started pacing. Kate couldn't bear the silence.

"I know I should have told you earlier, but I couldn't make up my mind what to do. It could be a hoax for all I know."

"Or it could be genuine. Have you asked your mother about it?"

"She's got dementia! She doesn't even know her own name."

Corcoran continued prowling around the small room, making her really uncomfortable. Kate felt a lump in her throat. *I will not get emotional, not at work.*

"Have you anyone who would know? Did you look for evidence of an adoption? Maybe there's something at your parents' house?"

"There's no one left alive who would know. Both my parents were only children. I have no aunties or uncles, no cousins. And there's something else, I dug out my original birth certificate and got the Documents guy in the Technical Bureau to look at it. He did it as a favour for me, under the radar. He says it's a fake, a good one but a fake. I'm not sure yet what that means. My father was a Garda, for fuck's sake! Would he really have taken part in some illegal baby-selling scheme?"

Kate's voice cracked, and she held back tears. Corcoran went quiet.

"Right," he said finally. "I'm sorry if it's a personal thing for you, but this woman, Bernie, is it? She was in St Mary's. She probably knew Billy Butler. You're going to have to speak to her."

"Does it have to be me?"

"She wants to talk to you, Kate; it's our way in. Put the personal stuff aside. Take Gardiner with you; he can ask the questions," said Corcoran.

He refolded the letter, handed it back, opened his office door and headed at speed down the corridor, Kate following.

"First, he needs to check out that chatroom or whatever it is. I'll get him onto it now. What's it called?"

"Donnybrookmarys, it's a Facebook group."

"Whatever...Gardiner can log on or join up, whatever the term is. It could be crucial."

Once they'd briefed him, Rory had news from the scene at St Mary's.

"They've found an annexe at the end of the garden behind a bunch of trees. It's got cots and baby stuff and a dormitory of sorts. It seems like it was the nursery."

"So...you'd expect that in a mother and baby home," said Kate.

"There's something else, a little garden behind the nursery...there's a burial plot."

"Jesus Christ, are we talking dead babies?" said Corcoran, and every head in the room turned. "How many?"

"There's a headstone; the techies counted seventeen names, just first names. All infants under three. They died at different dates between 1940 and 1989."

The room went quiet. Kate forgot to breathe. The words "dead babies" kept repeating in her head.

"Get those fucking nuns in here for questioning, tomorrow," said Corcoran. "This whole sorry mess is tied up with that place, and those women know more than they're saying."

Gardiner followed Kate and Corcoran back to his office, bringing a big cardboard box. It was filled to the brim with dusty leather-bound books, all foolscap size.

"What now?" said Corcoran, clearly disturbed by the latest discovery.

"These are record books from St Mary's, ledgers I think, going back to the 1940s."

"Anything useful in them?"

"I haven't had much time to look yet. They're full of names and addresses, dates of birth, payments, that sort of thing. Details of each of the girls and women who stayed there, and a little bit about their babies. Plus how much was paid to the nuns for their stay, and who paid it."

"Details of anyone we know? Our victims?"

"Irene Connolly and Deirdre McMahon were not in St Mary's. I'd say their involvement was in taking the babies to the States," said Kate.

"No reference to any of our victims so far," said Gardiner. "There is one strange thing though."

"Spit it out, lad," said Corcoran. Kate could see he was tiring; it had been a long day.

"Each ledger covers a period of one calendar year, dating from 1940 when the nursing home opened, right up until 1989 when it closed. Book after book, neatly handwritten in pen and ink."

Corcoran and Kate exchanged a knowing look.

"Billy Butler, the bookkeeper," said Kate. Corcoran nodded.

"There's one year missing," Rory Gardiner went on. "1968 isn't here."

This time Kate shot a panicked look at her boss.

"Is that the year...?"

"Yes," she said before he could finish the question.

Rory looked from one to the other, puzzled.

"What..." he asked.

Kate didn't answer.

"You two have a potential witness to interview," said Corcoran. "It's late now; leave it 'til the morning. Kate will fill you in then. You look bushed, Hamilton, go home and get a few hours' kip. Any luck with the French convent, Gardiner?"

"Not yet, but I'll keep pestering them," said Rory. "I'll be here for a while yet tonight. I can look at that Facebook group now."

Kate stood up, unwilling to step back even for a few hours, but achingly tired and a little shaky. Tomorrow she would tell Rory her story; for now she wanted him to find as much background on Bernie O'Toole and the Facebook group as possible.

"We need a list of everyone who joined, even if they're no longer active," said Kate, "plus any Friends and anyone who ever posted. Get onto Facebook Security. Tell them this is a murder enquiry and we're getting Digital Information Warrants. They might cough up."

"I've got a mate who works there, he won't help us, it's not his area, and he'd lose his job if he did," said Rory, "but he'll know who I should talk to."

"Do it, Gardiner," said Corcoran, "apply for the warrants, and contact your mate. We need to open up that group. Now go on, the two of you. I need to do some thinking."

## 29

K
ate left Rory Gardiner at his screen. He didn't even look tired while she was struggling to focus; was it an age thing? Tonight she felt every one of her forty-two years. It was nearly nine o'clock when she made it home, though the journey passed on autopilot. Greg was there; he'd been in London for a couple of days. He gave her a long hug she didn't want to end.

"How was London?"

"I liked it a lot; there's a good buzz."

He opened a bottle of red. Kate told him about the killing at St Mary's. Then the whole story, including Bernie O'Toole's letter, spilled out. He knew nothing of Ireland's dark social history.

"Your mom and dad loved you, Kate. You told me about your childhood. It was a pretty good one; don't let go of that."

"But what if it was built on a lie, on an illegal adoption... That's a bitter pill...if it's true..."

"You could take a DNA test."

Kate was taken aback; obvious as it seemed, the thought hadn't crossed her mind.

"Whoa, I'm not quite there yet, Greg. This woman could be lying through her teeth."

"What about the fake birth certificate? That's kinda convincing..."

"Maybe, but there could be another explanation, a clerical error at the Registry, something like that..." Her voice tailed off, she wasn't even convincing herself, but this wasn't the time to go there, not yet. "So, let's talk about something else, OK? This is a complete head-wreck. What did you do in London?"

"I went to the *Washington Post* bureau to meet the station head."

"Really, on your holidays? You're such a workaholic!"

"Strictly speaking, this wasn't entirely a vacation..." said Greg. "I've been meaning to tell you, but there just hasn't been the right moment. I've been offered a new posting, Europe correspondent."

Kate was so surprised she couldn't think of anything to say.

"It would be two years to start with, based in London," Greg went on. "I'd be just an hour away."

Kate took a moment to digest this.

"Are you going to accept it?" she asked, but she didn't get a straight answer.

"I liked the station head; she's a real character. I think we'd get along. It's a small operation, they've got stringers all over the UK and Europe, but I'd be covering the big stories."

"Wow, sounds busy."

"Yeah, but I like it that way. Not so busy that I couldn't be in Dublin every couple of weeks...or you could come to London...what do you think?"

This was big, but while her head was sounding alarm bells, Kate couldn't stop herself smiling.

"Do you want it?" she asked.

He smiled back.

"I want it," he said, "and I want you."

"Just every week or two though! You've already accepted it, haven't you?"

"Not yet, I wanted to run it by you first."

Kate didn't hesitate. "I think Europe is big enough for the two of us, don't you?"

Then they went to bed.

———

KATE WAS in the Murder Squad room by 8 am the next morning and found Gardiner already at his screen. He looked fresh, but she wondered if he'd been there all night.

"The stuff is coming in from France, downloading file by file. It's going to take a while before I get through it all," he said.

"Good, that means we'll have time to interview our witness," she said.

"What witness? Corcoran said you'd fill me in," said Rory.

"I'll give you the background en route. First I'll ring and see if she's available to talk to us."

Taking a deep breath, Kate dialled the number on the letter from Bernie O'Toole. The voice that answered was warm and strong, not as she'd imagined.

"I'm calling from Garda HQ. I'm a detective sergeant on the Murder Squad, Mrs O'Toole," said Kate.

"Is this about the murders?" Kate was taken aback.

"Yes, it is...how did you know?"

"I'm glad you called, Detective. I've been a bit worried and...afraid. I didn't know what to do about it..."

Kate finished the conversation by making arrangements to call to Bernie's address in Churchtown within the hour. She insisted on driving so she wouldn't have the headspace to get nervous. On the way she told Gardiner just how and why this woman was on their radar. He listened quietly.

"Do you believe she's your birth mother?"

It took Kate a while to answer.

"Look...I really don't know. I found my birth certificate. The Document guy in the Technical Bureau looked at it for me. Apparently it's a fake, a good one, but definitely a fake. They checked with the Registry of Births, and there's no corresponding entry."

"And your parents...?"

"My father died twenty years ago. My mother's got dementia. She barely recognises me. She does sometimes talk about the past. In fact, she's more lucid about things that happened years ago than the present. I haven't asked her about it. The truth is it's just not an easy conversation to start, even if she is gaga."

"How long have you known?"

"I got the letter about two months ago...kind of ignored it since. Then all this happened, and I couldn't keep quiet any longer. I told the boss yesterday – I thought he was going to bawl me out, but he didn't."

"It's a lead; if you look at it from his point of view, it's another lead," said Rory. "This woman could have some vital information for the enquiry."

"Exactly, and *you're* going to get it out of her. Any possible connection I might have to that place, and I don't for one minute believe it's anything but a case of mistaken identity, it can't compromise any future court case. You take her statement, OK. I'll just observe and take notes; then it's all above board. What did you get from the Facebook group?"

"So far, a lot. I've been able to identify most of the members. It's fucking astounding how much personal information people share. Don't they know how easy it is for someone to find out everything about them?"

"Clearly not, people are stupid; they overshare. So who's on it?"

"As far as I can see, there are a couple of dozen former patients, a few randomers who are interested in the whole history of mother and baby homes or just plain nosey, and some adoptees who believe they might have come from there. But here's the thing, the most important thing I found...Some of the flight crew posted on there, the ones who escorted the infants across the Atlantic by the planeload, including victims number one and two."

Kate almost stopped the car.

"And you tell me this last of all! Christ, Rory, that's huge! Both of them? It has to matter. What about the nuns? Are any of them in the group? And Billy Butler, was he?"

"We found no computers at the convent, and from what I hear, he wasn't the type to be online. But there is at least one poster who seems to know a hell of a lot about St Mary's; sounds like he or she could have worked there alright, could be a nun. He or she's got no profile details I can dig into, no pictures, no other Facebook groups or friends. They're using the chat feature to private message each other and to link up with people who are looking for specific information, so I can't say for sure."

"And our witness, Bernie?"

"She was an early member, says she's a mother who had a child there."

"Anyone else?"

"Not that I've managed to identify."

"My letter said there had been reunions?"

"Yes, over the last year, three adopted people located their birth mothers through the Facebook group. Some of them have moved offline since, but one posted a picture of their first meeting, mother and adopted child. It took place in the States. The rest of the group posted to congratulate them."

"What is it about that place...why are these people being targeted?"

The satnav had brought them to the suburbs without much delay; now Kate pulled the car into a spot outside the address Bernie O'Toole had given her.

"Try to keep my name out of it, Rory. I don't want her to know who I am just yet."

"Sure, I get that. You're in a really weird situation here; do you want me to go in alone?"

"No, I'm fine; let's just get it over with."

Bernie O'Toole had been waiting for them. The front door of the dormer bungalow opened before they could reach it.

"Detectives, come in, please. You're very welcome."

## 30

Inside the house was attractive; it looked to have been recently refurbished. Bernie led them into a large sitting room in the front of the house. It was a bright uncluttered space with a mixture of contemporary furniture and one or two quirky pieces that might have come from Asia, including some striking fabric cushions and a fabulous wall-hanging that looked Chinese. Bernie O'Toole was slim and well-dressed with an attractive smile. She looked to Kate to be in her early fifties, though her letter had mentioned that she was almost sixty.

There was already a tray with a coffee pot and biscuits on the table. The trio sat down. Kate let Rory Gardiner take the lead while she studied the woman in front of them. Bernie had a sleek blonde bob, expertly applied make-up, and expensive but delicate gold jewellery. She wore a cornflower blue cashmere jumper over grey jeans. Nothing in her physical presence looked familiar. Kate felt no instant recognition or connection, no déjà vu. Nonetheless, she was on edge, and each time the older woman's eyes alighted on her, Kate's discomfort grew. She had been careful not to disclose her name either on the phone or upon arrival. Bernie O'Toole accepted the oversight without question.

Gardiner began by asking her about the Facebook group "Donnybrookmarys".

"I think it started up about a year ago. I stumbled upon it around then anyway. I don't do a lot of social media, but I'm on Facebook. Mostly to keep in touch with my friends in England, I lived there for a long time," she said, "and it's nice to see what they're up to."

"What made you decide to join the group?"

"I was in St Mary's in Donnybrook a long time ago. So the name caught my eye...People were talking about being there...telling their stories, women who never got over the experience, never forgot that place. I haven't spoken about St Mary's in so many years, but it brought it all back. I suppose it felt good to talk to others who'd been through it...Then someone posted looking for their birth mother, and it was like the floodgates opened. Soon all the posts were about finding one another. Mothers searching for their children, children searching for their mothers."

"And did they? Find one another?" asked Rory.

"One or two did, I think. They posted pictures together; it was all very emotional."

"Did you find someone?" Kate couldn't help holding her breath.

"Not exactly, no." Bernie hesitated.

"Are you still active in the group?"

"Not at the moment. I wanted to think about it before I posted again. I've been a bit afraid."

Kate couldn't keep quiet any longer.

"Why are you afraid, Mrs O'Toole?"

"You'll think I'm being paranoid...but in the last few days with all these horrible murders happening...those two women, the one in Killiney and the other one down in

Kildare, the two that used to be air hostesses? Well, I'm almost sure they both posted on the site, little bits about the flights they took to the States with all the babies, even some pictures of them with the little ones. It suddenly occurred to me that putting my details out there might be...sort of risky."

Bernie smiled nervously, as if waiting to be told that there was nothing to be afraid of. When the reassurance didn't come, her smile faded.

Rory Gardiner glanced at Kate; she nodded to him to carry on.

"Tell me about Billy Butler," he asked.

"Poor Billy...he was there longer than anyone else. He used to say he was there 'man and boy'. The truth is he was more boy than man, like a big child. But he was a gentle soul. He mostly did the bookkeeping and a few odd jobs around the place. Us girls used to tease him a bit, and the nuns bossed him about like a dog, but he never complained. I was really sorry to hear he was dead. I hadn't realised he was still in St Mary's. I thought the place was long since empty."

"And how was it that you heard he had died?"

"One of the regulars in the group posted that he'd passed away. Billy Butler, St Mary's RIP was all it said. I suppose he must have been getting on; he was older than me anyway but only a few years, maybe sixty-four or five..."

Kate felt she had to intervene.

"I'm afraid Billy didn't exactly 'pass away' as you put it, Mrs O'Toole, not from old age anyway. We're treating his death as suspicious."

Kate was aware her words were a bit abrupt, and she could see Bernie O'Toole was shocked. Suddenly, the enormity of a possible third murder dawned on her.

"But that's three people dead...three who've been murdered! All connected to St Mary's. I remember the days when the Aer Lingus minibus would come to collect the babies. Those hostesses were so glamorous; we used to envy them in their smart uniforms."

Her voice was panicky.

"We're exploring the idea that there may be a connection between the victims; however, it's by no means certain, Mrs O'Toole."

Gardiner kept his voice calm and even. Bernie sat stock-still.

"Do you think we could have some more coffee, please? I've let mine go cold," Kate said.

Bernie got up, took the coffee tray and promised to be back in a couple of minutes. Before he could ask what was going on, Kate whispered urgently to Rory.

"The killer is finding his victims among the Facebook group; it's the only thing that makes sense, the only thing that connects them, well, that and St Mary's."

"I agree, it's his hunting ground. Anyone half-decent on a computer would be able to track down names and addresses from the personal data they've shared."

"There has to be a way to trace the killer; could we use Bernie to set a trap?"

"What do you mean?" Gardiner looked alarmed, but Kate was excited.

"If she could post something on the page that would flush him out, is there a way of tracing him...digitally, actually finding the location of the computer he's using?"

"There might be, I'd have to get the Cyber Crime Unit involved, but I think they could do it."

Bernie returned with the coffee. Sipping at fresh cups, they made small talk for a few minutes. The biscuits were home-made, and Rory complimented her on them, eliciting a proud smile and a bit of idle chat about baking, the price of shop-bought goods and Bernie's devotion to *The Great British Bake Off*. Gradually the colour returned to the older woman's cheeks. Kate nudged Rory. It was time to make his pitch.

"Mrs O'Toole, we think it's best if you stay off the Facebook page for the moment. It's not that we feel there is any threat to your safety, but until we can eliminate the other group members from our enquiries, it would be sensible for you to stay offline. However, to help us with our investigation, I'd like to have your login details. Would that be possible? And don't be disturbed if it looks like someone has posted in your name; it'll only be me, seeing if I can contact some of the other users."

Kate had to admire his tone; he managed to sound like it was the most natural thing in the world to assume the online identity of a witness in a multiple murder enquiry. Bernie went to find her laptop, saying she couldn't always remember her online details. Soon they were ready to leave, the vital login and password saved on Gardiner's phone, and for safety, in Kate's notebook. On the doorstep Gardiner handed Bernie his official contact card.

"If you think of anything else, call me, Mrs O'Toole, and any worries, just pick up the phone to HQ or the local guards."

Bernie looked expectantly at Kate, making her feel very uncomfortable.

"Do you have a card, Detective? It's Sergeant Hamilton, isn't it?"

Kate was taken aback but managed to hide it as she handed over her own card.

"Thank you, my dear, that will make me feel a bit less nervous. I'm putting on the house alarm the minute you're gone." She smiled and waved them off before shutting the front door very firmly.

The two detectives walked to their car silently, but as soon as the door was shut, they were rushing to speak.

"How did she...?"

"I don't know how she knew my name. I certainly didn't say it. Did you?"

"No, I didn't, I'm sure I didn't. You flashed your badge though; maybe she spotted it then..."

"She must have 20/20 vision to see it in a split second like that."

"Maybe she does; she wasn't wearing glasses. She knows who you are, and you were high profile on every news bulletin when you cracked that big case, so she knows what you look like."

"So she knew all the time I was the person she wrote that letter to...but she didn't let on. This bloody case just gets weirder and weirder..."

"She could have worked it out; that letter was what led us to her. She's sharp as a tack for a woman her age."

"Jesus, Rory! Do you know how patronising you sound? A woman her age! Most of the CEOs of big global companies are her age. Some of the richest and most powerful people in the world are her age or older. Only difference is they're all *men*. Nobody questions *their* mental abilities."

Kate was unreasonably annoyed, and Gardiner had the good sense to stay quiet. At headquarters he went off to the Cyber Crime Unit. Kate found Corcoran and reported back on the interview.

"So you think we can flush him out?" he asked.

"I don't know, it's worth a try..."

"Let's see what the Cyber lads say. If they can pinpoint his location, we'll need to have every available unit on standby; this will have to be co-ordinated. What if he's in fucking Donegal? We can't have every Garda in the country standing by."

"I know, I get that. It might get us nowhere, or it could narrow the search down..."

"What about this O'Toole woman?" said Corcoran. "Do you think she's safe?"

"I've asked the local lads in Dundrum to do a regular drive-by," Kate said.

"Tell them to keep it to unmarked units, or she'll be completely freaked out." Corcoran sat silent for a while; finally he stood up with purpose.

"Right, let's get the team together. I think we have a real lead on our killer, and they need to know. Squad room in five minutes, get them all in."

## 31

There was a weariness in the room. It had been a week since the first murder; newspaper headlines screamed from some of the desks, "GARDAI CLUE-LESS IN MURDER SPREE", "WOMEN LIVE IN FEAR", "JUSTICE MINISTER SENDS FOR GARDA CHIEF".

Corcoran called for quiet, and the team complied.

"We have a line of enquiry, finally. We're focused on the man who we think left the murder scene at St Mary's. Enquiries in the local pub have given us a loose description. Could be an American, thirty-five to forty-five years old, tall and well built. Unfortunately we haven't been able to source decent CCTV of him. Hamilton – fill them in on the Facebook thing."

Kate stood up.

"Apart from the woman in Rathgar, we've established all the victims have a connection to St Mary's. It was a private mother and baby home up until the 1990s. Irene Connolly and Deirdre McMahon, our first two victims, escorted the babies for adoption, almost certainly illegal adoption, to the US on Aer Lingus flights all through the sixties and seventies.

Billy Butler worked at the convent for some fifty years. Somehow this has made them targets for our killer."

"What's this Facebook thing?" asked one of the detectives.

"Some of the former residents at St Mary's set up a group about a year ago. We think that's how the killer found his victims. With no hit on the DNA or fingerprints, we're going to use the group in a bid to flush him out. Gardiner, how did you get on with the Cyber guys?"

Rory Gardiner flushed slightly as all eyes in the room turned to him. He wasn't used to this kind of attention, but as he spoke, Kate was glad to see his confidence grow.

"It's complicated, but they can do it. We need to post something to the page that looks and sounds like our witness, Mrs O'Toole, something that he won't be able to ignore. If he's on there and responds, we should be able to trace his IP address."

Corcoran spoke then.

"And will that give us a location? Will it ping like a mobile phone does on a cell mast?"

"Essentially yes, once the Cyber team have set up the trace. It's not something they do all the time, more of a hacker's technique. Probably not strictly legal."

"Fuck legal," someone muttered from the back of the room; no one disagreed.

"Right," said Jim Corcoran, "we need to alert every station sergeant in the country. If we do get a location, it could be anywhere; they all need to know that if we shout, they jump. Airport police are on the lookout, but the description is too vague. He could easily have got past them. If he's still in Ireland, we've a slim chance. In the morning Gardiner will post on the Facebook page. Hamilton and Gardiner, you two need to work out what that message will be; the rest of you go home now and be back here at 6 am. We'll draw up a plan – I want you all in place at key access points north, south, and west of the city, so we've got the whole Greater Dublin area covered if we get a hit. We'll cover the city centre from here."

The team dispersed then, and Kate and Gardiner spent another hour poring over the Facebook page. In the end they decided Bernie's post would go in the comments on the post that announced Billy Butler's death.

"Poor old Billy, who could have done such a thing? I need to talk to someone. I think I know what's going on."

Kate barely slept. Greg was in London, finalising the arrangements for his move. The apartment felt wrong without him. As the night dragged on, she vowed to put it on the market as soon as the case was over. It didn't feel like home anymore; maybe it never had. She would move back into her mother's house. It had lain empty now for a year, and she could never bring herself to rent it out. Too many echoes. A few weeks back in the house where she grew up would give her time to breathe, to listen to the memories, to find the truth.

By 8 am the next morning the trap was set. Two of the Cyber Unit's officers had taken up residence in the Murder Squad room, complete with state-of-the art laptops and head-phones. One of them looked impossibly young to Kate. The second officer at least had the look of someone who shaved, but they were both uncommunicative and nerdy looking, exactly as she'd imagined they'd be. Kate left Gardiner to deal with the Cybercops, as Corcoran dubbed them.

In his office they reviewed the evidence from each crime scene. They were both nervy and quiet. Impatiently, she opened her own laptop and logged on to Facebook. She had joined the site only the day before, but it gave her access to the donnybrookmarys group. Whoever had set it up knew little about privacy settings; anyone could see the page, including Gardiner's post using Bernie O'Toole's login. No one had responded yet.

"What if he doesn't bite?" she said.

"We'll find another way to trace him," said Jim. "There's something here, there has to be."

Kate's laptop was loading old posts on the donnybrook-marys page, going back to the group's inception a year earlier; it was taking a while. She started going through the photos people had uploaded. Many were old black-and-white pictures, sweet poses of chubby toddlers in the arms of beaming couples. One photo showed an Aer Lingus hostess carrying a small boy down the steps of a plane. At the bottom stood a welcoming party – a well-dressed couple and a priest. People had scanned in pictures of birth certificates, old letters and even passports, featuring yet more apple-cheeked chil-dren. Kate stared at the array of little faces, then the birth certificates, all uncannily like her own dodgy one. Then a passport caught her eye; it was an old one with a green cover. The poster had scanned in every page individually; Kate went through them all. The sixth page was headed:

*THIS PASSPORT IS GOOD FOR THE FOLLOWING COUNTRIES:*
*ALL COUNTRIES.*

This was repeated in Irish and French:

*GACH AON TIR*
*TOUS LES PAYS*

At the bottom of the page, there was a stamp:

*PASSPORT OFFICE DUBLIN*

There was a signature, Phyllis F. Whelan. Idly she wondered if every passport was individually signed.

Searching back through the photos, she found another passport uploaded by an adoptee. There it was again, Phyllis F. Whelan. Suddenly she stood up, almost dropping her laptop.

"The crime scene photos from Rathgar, where are they?"

"Why, what is it?"

"I don't know, but something rings a bell. I need to see the pictures." She set off to the Op Room at a run, Corcoran following. Apart from Gardiner and the Cybercops, the place was empty.

"Nothing yet, boss," said Rory, without turning his head from his computer screen.

Kate ignored him. Scanning the Murder Wall, she couldn't place the picture she wanted, but she soon found the sheaf of photos taken in the Rathgar house. Quickly she sorted through them, casting each one aside.

"There, I've found it!" She was almost shouting, but only Corcoran took notice.

"For fuck's sake, Hamilton, what?"

She thrust one of the photos in his face. "Look at the mantelpiece; look at the photo frame," she said triumphantly.

"It's a cutting, looks like a wedding photo from a newspaper. That's our third victim, I reckon, and presumably her husband," he said.

"Read the caption."

"Mr Robert Berry and his bride Phyllis Berry nee Whelan after their wedding at St Audoen's Church, Dublin," he read.

"Phyllis J. Whelan, that's the signature on the passports, the baby passports! It has to be her. It's *her* connection to St Mary's. She signed the passports for the babies to be sent abroad. *That's* why she was murdered, because of her part in the baby trade."

"Jesus Christ, you could be right. She wasn't on the Facebook page, but she was involved. We're going to have to contact the authorities and find out what she did. I know she was a retired civil servant, but were they legal passports or fakes? Was it legit or a lucrative sideline?"

"Whichever it was, it seems like it got her killed," said Kate.

"We have lift-off," said Rory Gardiner. "Someone's posted on the page."

"What did he post?" asked Kate.

"He asked Bernie what she knew about Billy's death. Made it sound like an innocent question, a sort of 'are you OK, hon' question," said Gardiner.

"Do you think it's our guy?"

"It's someone who uses an alias, one of the few I haven't been able to identify. I think it's our man, I've studied his posts, and he always seems to be asking questions, fishing for info. He calls himself the Historian, claims to be writing a paper on mother and baby homes, but I wasn't able to establish any kind of professional credentials for him; he's a ghost."

Kate and Corcoran stood over the Cybercops as streams of numbers and codes ran across their screens. The two officers ignored them, their fingers flying across the keyboards.

"It could be our man; he's taken the bait," said Kate. "Send a vague response, Rory; we need to keep him online."

Rory Gardiner was still logged in to Facebook. Quickly he typed: "I'm so so sad about poor Billy, he was such a softie" and added a sad face emoji.

"How long?" asked Corcoran, but the two techies ignored him. Minutes passed. To Kate it felt like hours. Finally they stopped the furious typing, and a Google map appeared on one screen. A small green symbol flickered on and off near the centre.

"Where? Where is he?"

"Looks like he's south of the city, but not far," said the younger officer. "That's Dun Laoghaire. I know that place, it's a hotel near the seafront. The Royal Hotel. That's where the computer he's posting from is located." He sat back, almost breathless from the effort. Without a word of thanks, the detectives were out the door in seconds, leaving the two Cybercops to high-five each other in the empty squad room.

## 32

A n excitable Lithuanian receptionist told detectives that their suspect had left the hotel barely half an hour earlier, but in the lobby of the five-star Royal Hotel, a barely concealed chaos reigned. Staff were trying to maintain a professional attitude, but it wasn't every day they had a visit from Dublin's elite Murder Squad, and in such numbers. The hotel and its grounds were in lockdown. No one was allowed to leave, and everyone entering the premises was stopped and questioned.

"We've lost him, I'm sure of it," said Corcoran, pacing on the deep pile carpet, frustration deepening the lines of exhaustion on his face.

"We'll get a lead from his room – he doesn't know we're onto him. He'll have left something we can use," said Kate, "and at least we know what he looks like now."

CCTV from the hotel's many cameras had finally revealed the face of the man they believed was Thomas Larkin, aka the Historian. In footage from the residents' lounge, a Wi-Fi hotspot where a number of PCs were available for guests' use, they had located clear shots of a dark-haired man in black clothing, logged on at the exact time when the Facebook trap set by Rory Gardiner had brought Thomas Larkin out into the open. The suspect was the only occupant of the lounge at the time, so there was no mistaking it. He had checked in a week earlier using an American passport in the name of Tim Larsson. This information had been sent to the officers back at HQ, and international searches were underway for background on Larsson. Behind the reception desk in a discreet corner, Kate was fast-forwarding through days and hours of CCTV footage to see if she could pick him up again. With a couple of detectives and two Gardai from the local station, Corcoran was supervising the search of the hotel. The Technical Bureau had taken up camp in room 212, Larsson's bolthole. So far the search of his room had yielded nothing, but Gardiner was probing the PC the suspect had used to see if anything could be gleaned from its history.

"I'm going to talk to the cabbies on the rank down the road; he may have taken a taxi somewhere," said Corcoran, striding out the opulent Victorian front door, to the annoyance of several guests waiting in line to be allowed to leave. Already excitement at the novelty of a police investigation had worn thin. Now the tourists just wanted to get on with their vacation unimpeded by a murder hunt, however thrilling.

"I've got a round of golf booked for two o'clock, officer, will I be outta here in time?" asked a portly American wearing yellow trousers and a pink check sweater. Corcoran didn't answer.

Kate's eyes were tiring already; she blinked rapidly to keep focus, but was glad of the break when her phone vibrated in her pocket. Pausing the pictures racing by on the screen, she scanned the text message. It was from Bernie O'Toole, her would-be birth mother. Kate frowned; she had deliberately put the whole question of her birth to the back of her mind, deciding for now to treat Bernie as just another witness. She was finding it difficult to know just how to relate to this woman who claimed to be her mother, but who was also directly involved in the case.

> Katie, I need to see you. Please come now
> Bernie x

This was annoying; she of all people should know the scale and importance of the case; how could she expect Kate to drop everything just like that? And why call her Katie? *That is just plain odd. It was one thing to find out late in life that you were adopted and had an actual mother as opposed to the poor demented woman who claimed that title. It was quite another for that so-called birth mother to use pet names and endearments like that troublesome kiss at the end of the text.*

"Any joy?" said Corcoran, standing behind her and making her jump. *Jesus Christ, for a big man he moves quietly!*

"Nothing significant yet. How about the taxi rank, anything there?"

"Nope, none of the drivers remembered the American, either this morning or anytime recently. Forget the CCTV for now; we'll get one of the civvies back at HQ to go through it. Export the files to them, and while you're on, get them to check hire-car firms for the suspect; that might be how he's getting around. Come on, Hamilton, I need you with me."

Kate set off the transfer of files to HQ and, having checked in with the CSIs in room 212, who had yet to find anything useful, joined Corcoran in his car. They left two junior officers to take statements from the impatiently waiting guests. Once they'd provided those, the officers were told to let them leave.

"Where are we going?" Kate asked.

"I don't know, but I'm fed up standing around in that

place. We've found damn all on Larkin or Larsson. If he's on foot, he might just be around here somewhere."

"He could have got a Dart or a bus; he could even have taken a ferry to Holyhead from here," said Kate.

"Thanks for raining on my parade! Why would he have left his luggage behind? I don't think he's fled the country. We've asked for CCTV from the bus, rail and ferry companies. It will be hours before we get our hands on it. The local guards are talking to any nearby businesses with cameras. As usual, half of them don't work. We have to try something, or I'll blow a gasket. We're closer than we've ever been to this bastard. I can't sit on my hands. Look around you, Kate – this is a pretty seaside town; he might just be walking the pier."

Kate's phone vibrated again. Annoyed, she pulled it from her pocket.

"Is that HQ? Have they found something?"

"No, it's Bernie O'Toole again."

"Our witness?"

"Yes, her. I never discussed the letter with her. I let Rory do the questioning, and he kept it focused on the case. Now all of a sudden she's sent me five texts in the space of an hour."

As they cruised the streets of Dun Laoghaire, each scanning the faces of passers-by, Kate updated Jim on her personal enquiries.

"I double-checked my birth certificate. There's no official record that matches it. My parents lied to me...all my life."

Corcoran could hear the catch in her voice, and his own was gentle when he spoke.

"People get desperate, Kate...when they can't have kids of their own. They'll do anything for a baby. Don't judge them too harshly."

Kate didn't trust herself to speak. Her phone pinged

again; wearily she swiped the screen and read the latest message from Bernie O'Toole.

"That's bloody odd," she said.

"What?"

"She's stalking me! Three texts in a row. This one is signed Mam, with a kiss! She's gone mad." Kate laughed unhappily. "Not only do I appear to have two mothers, but both of them are mental!"

Corcoran glanced at Kate; it looked to him like she didn't know whether to laugh or cry.

"She's trying to tell you something, Kate," he said.

"She's trying to be my bloody mother, and I have one already, thanks, even if she is completely gaga!"

"Don't obsess about it now. I need you focused. When the case is over, you can take some time off and do whatever you need to about this woman."

"She's part of it though..."

Kate paused mid-sentence.

"Stop the car, NOW!" she said.

Corcoran stood on the brakes. The car behind screeched to a halt just inches from their bumper, and a line of traffic quickly formed behind them.

"She wants me there; she wants me at her house now BECAUSE HE'S THERE! It's him...it's Larkin or Larsson or whatever his name is, he's found Bernie O'Toole, and he's going to kill her too."

"Where? Where does she live?" Corcoran said tensely over the cacophony of horns rising behind them. Then he punched on the siren and blue flashing tail lights, put the car into gear and set off in a screech of tyres, on the wrong side of the road.

"Churchtown, she lives in Churchtown," said Kate. Her heart thumped painfully in her chest.

"Anville Crescent, number 78. It's about twenty minutes from here. What'll I do? Will I get a squad car there?"

Kate struggled to control the panic in her voice.

"Yes and no." Corcoran swerved a cyclist and steered the car through a set of red lights with barely a glance to the left or right.

"Get an Emergency Response unit on standby, but tell them to hang back, out of sight. If Larsson is there, we don't want to spook him."

## 33

Bernie O'Toole wasn't great with religion, but you couldn't be rude to a priest, or a tourist for that matter, not in Bernie's book, anyway. *Sure wasn't the one to be pitied and the other to be pampered; if it weren't for the tourists, wouldn't the country be banjaxed altogether.* When the handsome American knocked on her door, she was about to settle down with a strong coffee, some still warm lemon drizzle cake and her favourite soap on the TV. She invited the stranger in and hoped she could press record on her Skybox without him noticing, and that he wouldn't stay too long or expect a big donation for the parish.

"What brings you to these shores, Father?" she asked.

"Well, actually I'm Irish, ma'am. At least I was born here but raised in the States."

He had an accent Bernie recognised as East Coast American, clipped not drawling, almost refined for a Yank, she thought.

"Oh really, isn't that nice, Father. So are you working here, or is it a holiday you're on?"

The American sipped his coffee. "Kind of a working vacation, ma'am," he said.

"Oh, so you're with the parish, are you? I knew there was a great shortage of priests alright. There's hardly a curate to be found the length and breadth of the country. The last funeral I was at, the priest was from Nigeria, a lovely man. He said he was a sort of travelling pastor, filling in here and there all over the country. Is that what you're doing?"

"I have been moving around, yes, but my main purpose has been to trace my family here in Ireland, ma'am."

"Really? Isn't that marvellous altogether." Bernie's voice rose a little, and she found herself on her feet without having planned it. There was something about this priest that didn't fit, and she wanted a moment to herself to work it out.

"Let me get you some fresh coffee, Father; sure that one must be cold by now. I have one of those fancy coffee machines I got as a present; makes a great cup, but too small by far. I'll go and top it up. You relax there and make yourself comfortable. Oh, and look out for the cat; she's a bit on the vicious side."

Bernie had the cup out of her visitor's hand before he could protest. In the kitchen she took out her phone and began a text. Kate Hamilton was the first person she thought of, but what would she say?

"I really don't need more coffee, ma'am." Bernie hadn't heard the priest follow her.

"I'll just top up mine, then, Father, and I'll be right in to you." Bernie smiled a smile she wasn't feeling and turned round to find her visitor standing very close. Silently he took her mobile from her hand and read the text she'd begun.

"Who's Kate?"

"My...daughter. She's my daughter; she's coming by for the afternoon. That's why I made the cake."

She might be shaking inside, but Bernie had a momentary surge of self-satisfaction at her own quick-wittedness. Her fear of the man in her home was escalating, but he wasn't going to find her an easy prey. She took back her phone from his hand and carried on tapping out a message.

"Tell me about St Mary's," said the priest. Bernie felt her chest tighten and fought to keep the fear from her words.

"Who are you?" she asked.

"I'm a nobody, a foundling, a reject. I'm a dirty little secret from this shithole of a country."

Bernie winced and backed as far away as the confines of the kitchen would allow. *No priest would use that kind of language.* He held out his hand for her phone.

"Tell her not to come; tell her you're too busy to see her."

"Why, I'd like her with me...I'll tell you all about St Mary's, but Kate should be here."

The man's face darkened, and he moved towards her. Bernie stood her ground.

"Why?"

"It's her story too," she said, and pressed Send on her text.

---

THE ARMED UNIT took up their positions around Anville Crescent. Crouched behind hedges and garden walls, there were eight marksmen in total, not one with a clear line of sight inside number 78. Corcoran and Kate had made the journey in just over fifteen minutes, and the Emergency Response Unit had arrived a little later, sirens silenced some half a mile out from the target, on Corcoran's orders. A heated argument was going on behind the police cordon.

"I have to go in now," said Kate.

"Not until a negotiator gets here, and not without a stab vest and a firearm."

"But we don't know if he's even in there."

"He could be inside; we have to be prepared for that."

"Bernie just texted me again; she's still alive, I'm sure of it."

"He could be using her phone."

Kate couldn't argue with that. Reluctantly she strapped on the stab vest and a holster loaded with a small automatic. One of the plain-clothes Gardaí who had been escorting Bernie O'Toole's next-door neighbours, an elderly couple and a young mum with a baby, from their homes handed her a pale blue baggy jumper.

"We got it from one of the washing lines, it's a bit big, but that'll disguise the vest and the holster," said Corcoran.

Kate checked her reflection in the car window; it was passable with her jeans if you didn't look too closely. She pulled her hair loose from its ponytail to chime with the casual look. At that moment another car drew up. Kate recognised the officer who emerged as one of the few hostage negotiators on the force, Frank Murphy. They'd been on a training course together. He walked towards her.

"You sure about this?" Frank asked. "We could set up comms with the suspect and try to talk him out."

"I have to go in, and I'm well prepared, you know that," said Kate. "Wouldn't it be funny if this was all just Bernie being a bit doolally," she said to Corcoran.

"Don't do anything stupid, Hamilton. Any sign of a threat – use it, do you hear me?"

Kate had never seen him look so stressed. Stepping out into the open, she rounded the crescent-shaped road and headed for number 78. *If this were a movie, there'd be snipers on every rooftop, and I'd be wearing a wire so that my squad could hear every word inside the house.* But it wasn't a movie, and all they had was the hastily convened and slightly nervy ERU, more used to thwarting bank robberies than stalking lone-wolf killers in suburbia.

The doorbell echoed in the quiet house. Were they too late? Had Bernie already been brutalised and stabbed in her own home? The door opened.

"You must be Katie. Bernie says to come on in."

It was the dog collar that threw her. God, she should have rehearsed what she'd say when she came face to face with Thomas Larkin, aka Tim Larsson. Now all she could think of was, *That's how he gained access to the victims' homes! The dog collar.*

"Father..." She stumbled on the word.

"Please come in – we're just having a coffee, your mom and me."

## 34

Bernie O'Toole looked pale and wide-eyed, and Kate was surprised by the tight hug she gave her.

"Katie love, I'm so glad you came. We've got so much to talk about; come and sit beside me. Let me introduce Father Thomas Larkin; he's over here to find his roots."

Larkin had followed them into the sitting room. Kate sat down beside Bernie, who had kept hold of her hand and now clasped it tightly in her own. Larkin sat on the sofa opposite, but he wasn't relaxed; he sat upright, leaning his elbows on his knees with his hands clasped under his chin.

"Katie's a civil servant, aren't you, love," said Bernie. "She works for the Revenue Commissioners, or is it the Health Service Executive, one of those government departments anyway, isn't it?"

Kate had taken advantage of Bernie's excitable chatter to observe Larkin. Dark haired and lean, he was tall and broad shouldered, handsome in a severe way. She would never be able to overpower him on her own, but the automatic was a comforting lump under her armpit. The curtains had been drawn, and several table lamps were lit. Kate wondered if that

had been Larkin's doing, or whether Bernie usually had them
that way in mid-afternoon. On the table three kitchen knives
were lined up precisely, like surgical instruments on the
white linen cloth. It was a startling image, but Kate managed
to keep her face neutral.

"Oh, Bernie, you keep forgetting. I'm with the Depart-
ment of Health, senior clerical officer, grade five. Not very
interesting, Father, but it pays the rent!"

Kate smiled. Larkin's face remained closed and
impassive.

"Kate, you won't believe this, but Thomas was born in St
Mary's too. He's been asking me all about it," said Bernie.

She seemed to be struggling to keep her voice even. Kate
realised the woman beside her was terrified. Had Larkin
threatened her already?

"Oh my goodness, that's amazing, Bernie. What a coincidence."

"What year?" said Larkin, and Kate tried to identify the
origin of his accent.

"I'm sorry?" she said.

"What year were you born?"

"Nineteen sixty-eight," said Kate, keeping her voice bright.
At all costs she wanted to keep him calm; maybe she could
talk him into leaving the house, away from Bernie and into
the trap that awaited him outside.

"Me too, 1968 – the same year I was born. Same year, same
place. Your mom didn't say a lot about St Mary's. How much
do you know?"

"Not much, not much at all. It's not long since Bernie and
I met, and we haven't had a lot of time to talk, have we?" Kate
pulled her hand from Bernie's clammy grasp and loosely put
her arm across the older woman's shoulders. She needed
both hands free, but she wanted to give her some reassurance
too.

"I think you've got some talking to do," said Larkin, making no attempt to disguise the coldness in his voice.

Kate was acutely conscious that Corcoran and the armed units outside would soon grow impatient.

"Maybe you could come back another day, Father. Bernie and I had plans for today."

"You could pop in tomorrow, and I'll be better prepared for you..." said Bernie.

Larkin stood up suddenly and turned away. Both women stiffened. Kate slipped her hand inside the baggy jumper and unclipped the holster, the metal of the automatic weapon comforting in her palm. Larkin walked to the table and, with his back to them, spoke.

"I've come a long way, done a lot of things...to get here. I need to hear about that place, and I need to hear it now."

He turned back towards them with one of the knives in his right hand. Bernie gasped and put her hand to her mouth. Kate took a deep breath. This wasn't the time to blow her cover; she pretended to be shocked.

"Oh my goodness, Bernie, why did you leave those kitchen knives lying out? Father Thomas could cut himself. You can see he's upset!"

Jumping up from the sofa, Kate walked quickly to Larkin, keeping her expression friendly and unknowing.

"Let me put those things away. I can't think why Bernie left them out," she said, pointing to the two kitchen knives on the table, and with her free hand gestured for Larkin to hand over the third.

"She can be a bit forgetful, you know," she said in a conspiratorial whisper.

He looked directly into her face.

"Sit down. Let's leave these right where they are."

Kate feigned puzzlement with Larkin's rudeness, but backed off and sat on the opposite sofa, as instructed. There was no need to let him know she was anything but a pushover. She would need the element of surprise if she had to tackle him. Larkin sat down, and Kate realised she'd made a dangerous tactical error. Now he had the knife, *and* he was right next to Bernie. Fuck! She should have drawn her weapon and arrested him at the front door, when Corcoran and the others could have swooped in to pick him up. She forced a bright tone into her voice, if only for Bernie's sake.

"Come on, Bernie, let's give Father Thomas what he wants. I'd like to hear about St Mary's too."

Larkin laid the knife down on the low coffee table between them. Bernie turned her face away from the shining blade and began her story. Kate couldn't help but be fascinated, though her mind was racing with escape strategies and fears.

"It wasn't such a bad place, you know," Bernie began almost defensively. "There were other ones, the mother and baby homes. They were much more harsh. They were cruel, horrible places; at least St Mary's was not like that. I won't say we were lucky, but because it was a private clinic...our parents paid, you know, quite a lot of money, even back then, to keep us in St Mary's. Being a private clinic, we weren't made to do laundry or anything like that; it was a bit like boarding school. Boarding school with bumps!" Bernie laughed nervously. "Most of us knew what that was like; we were used to nuns and all that God-bothering. Oh sorry, Father, no disrespect meant. That's what we called it when the nuns weren't listening. We had daily Mass and prayers morning noon and night."

Larkin's expression was stony.

"Tell me about the girls. How many were there in the winter of 1967 and 1968?"

"Oh, I'd say there were no more than a dozen, at most fourteen."

"How long did they, did you, stay there? How long before, and how long after the birth?" Kate asked, anxious to hurry up Bernie's account, worried about the armed pack surrounding the house.

"That depended, some girls had their babies and left straight away; some stayed six months or a year to mind them, until...until...they took them away."

Bernie looked stricken. A tear rolled down her cheek. Larkin stood up and started pacing. He was getting agitated. Kate needed to divert attention from Bernie.

"What date is your birthday?" Kate asked him.

"February 16, 1968. That's what I've been told, but my birth certificate is a fake, so who knows?"

Kate's heart skipped a beat. Larkin put his hand inside his jacket and took out a small leather-bound notebook. He started flicking through the pages of handwritten notes.

"I was born on February 16 too," Kate said.

Larkin stopped his pacing and came back to sit on the edge of the sofa next to Bernie.

"That's kinda weird, so you and my mother gave birth on the same day?" His voice was a mixture of elation and anger. "Tell me about my mother."

Bernie raised a tear-stained face.

"Her name was Rose...or Rose Mary as the nuns called her."

"The convent names," said Larkin.

"What do you mean?" asked Kate.

"We all had a convent name; mine was Agnes. They said I was a disgrace to Saint Bernadette, so they gave me Agnes. As saints go, she wasn't so popular, and I wouldn't be sullying her name."

"Tell me about my fucking mother," Larkin growled; then he took a handgun from inside his jacket and pointed it at them. Bernie gasped. Kate just stared at the Glock. She had thought she had the advantage. Not anymore. Suddenly the Sig Sauer in her holster was much less comforting. At close range, either weapon would be lethal. *Mutually assured destruction.* Kate's phone vibrated in her pocket.

"Leave it," he said, but Kate already had the phone up to her ear. She held up a palm to Larkin, to stall any move.

"Hi, Jim, I'm just here with Bernie in Churchtown. What's the story?"

Larkin got up and started pacing again.

"Situation report, Kate?"

It was the hostage negotiator, his voice even and quiet.

"I'll be a little while yet, Jim; we're just having a bit of a chat."

"Is he armed?"

"Yes, of course I'll pass on your regards to Bernie."

"Corcoran wants you out of there in the next fifteen minutes."

"Oh, I forgot he was coming round today. I'll be about half an hour, Jim, OK?" Larkin was standing over her now.

"I'll let you go now, love, and I'll see you later. Bye." Kate looked up at Larkin, the gun hung loosely in his right hand, like he'd been carrying one his whole life.

"My boyfriend, Jim," said Kate as Larkin held his hand out, "he was just wondering how long I'll be." Reluctantly she handed over the phone.

Larkin returned to pacing. He seemed to be unable to sit still.

"Keep talking," he said.

"Your mother's name was Rosie Jackson," said Bernie. He stopped pacing.

"Shit, I knew it – she's the one I couldn't find."

"Sorry?" said Bernie.

"She's the only one I couldn't get a lead on. Who was she? Get a move on. I'm tired of you droning on."

There was now no doubt in Kate's mind, Thomas Larkin was the killer who'd been terrorising the city for over a week. Bernie looked at her, and the sight of the older woman's anxious face made Kate suddenly angry.

"Don't speak to her like that, and why have you got a gun? Priests in this country don't generally come armed," she said.

All three of them seemed taken aback by her words. Kate was much slighter than Larkin but almost as tall, and her sudden challenge made him step back. It was totally against her training, but Kate was angry, and nothing was going to stop her.

"Put that bloody thing down and stop threatening us, or you're never going to get what you want. Just who the hell are you, and what are you doing here?"

Larkin glared.

"He's your brother, Kate...your twin brother," said Bernie quietly.

---

CORCORAN WAS LIKE A CAGED LION. Kate had been in the house over ten minutes. One of the ERU snipers had reported seeing a man matching Larkin/Larsson's description open the front door. Corcoran had instructed the marksmen to close in on the house. With the curtains drawn, the occupants couldn't see the approaching Gardai, but that worked both ways. They knew nothing of what was going on inside. He was rapidly running out of patience, and the negotiator's phone call to Kate hadn't helped.

"How did she sound?"

"She was calm, cheerful. She's obviously not disclosed her identity to Larkin. That means she still has the upper hand."

"Is he armed?"

"I think so; she said yes when I asked."

"Then she doesn't have the upper hand; he could easily overpower her."

"She's got a firearm, and from what we know, his weapon of choice is a blade."

"Not helping, Frank, not helping at all," Corcoran said grimly. "Set up the listening device; we have to know what's going on in there."

Two of the ERU officers moved slowly and quietly towards the house. In black from head to toe they carried machine pistols, and as dusk approached, they stayed in the shadows of the hedges and trees dotted around the quiet estate. One carried a small metal case. As they neared the house, they went down on their bellies in the garden, moving quickly to the base of the big picture window. One placed a tiny magnetic device on the pane of glass above his head while the other trained his weapon on the window. Corcoran put on an earpiece and winced at the burst of static that followed. The Garda lying beneath the window moved some controls on the small electronic unit. The muffled sound of voices came through. Next to Corcoran, the newly arrived High Tech surveillance officer pointed a heat-seeking camera at the house.

"Three heat sources, two on the move, one static."

"I can't make out what they're saying; try another position," Corcoran said into his radio. The prone officer gave a thumbs-up signal and began inching towards the far end of the window frame. He placed a second device right against the frame, where he could see a small gap in the curtain.

"Three voices, I can hear three. Thank God," said Corcoran. "All units hold your positions. We'll give her a bit more time to bring him out; otherwise we're going in."

## 35

"What did you just say?"

As one Kate and Larkin had turned to Bernie, their faces shocked. Larkin was the first to speak. Tears raked Bernie's cheeks.

"I think you two had better sit down, and I'll tell you about poor Rosie." Kate made sure she got the spot next to Bernie this time. He took his seat opposite, laying the Glock on the sofa beside his right hand.

"But you told me *you* were my mother," said Kate.

"Not exactly, Kate. I was desperate to meet you. I'm sorry I lied."

Larkin interrupted.

"Get to the point – Rosie Jackson," he almost spat the name out, "and this had better be good."

Bernie took a deep breath and began.

"She was my best friend at St Mary's, though I only knew her for a few weeks. She was the youngest of us all, only fourteen, I think. Just a child herself, really; she hardly knew what was happening to her..."

"How did she..." Kate found herself desperate to know more. "I mean, surely even at fourteen, she'd know..."

Bernie interrupted her.

"Rosie was very naïve; she didn't have a boyfriend. She was...she was a victim herself..."

"You mean...she was raped?" said Kate.

For a second she couldn't get her head around it all. She was trying to keep a grip on the situation, to get to the point where she could end it peacefully, get Larkin into custody and Bernie to safety, but every word that Bernie said sent her mind reeling.

"Yes, she was attacked...by her own first cousin."

*Christ*, thought Kate, *the woman isn't sugaring the pill. That's what a loaded gun to your head will do, every time.* Larkin was silent, his head bent.

"Go on, Bernie; we need to know," said Kate, surprised by her own use of the word "we".

"I'll tell you all I know about your birth. It was the day the Archbishop came; we'd been getting ready for weeks. The nuns were up to ninety with nerves and excitement. Anyway the 'great man' arrived. He was a sour-faced old bastard, and I've hated him ever since. He had just come in the front door, and we were all lined up like toy soldiers when poor Rosie's waters broke, there and then in front of him. The nuns almost lost their minds with embarrassment. We were all whisked away out of sight, and Rosie went off to the sick bay."

Kate thought she heard a sound at the window. Bernie and Larkin didn't appear to have noticed.

"What happened?" asked Larkin. Bernie wiped her eyes and sniffed loudly, but the tears kept coming.

"We could hear her, the rest of us girls, we could hear poor Rosie scream." Kate was only half listening as she strained to see if the noise outside would be repeated. Larkin was staring at Bernie.

"We'd heard girls scream in labour before, of course we had, though the nuns didn't like it. But this was different. Much, much worse. We were so scared for her. The nuns were in a holy panic. Between the Archbishop having his tea in the parlour, and Rosie's screams sounding up and down the corridors, it was chaos. Then the doctor came and an ambulance, sirens wailing and all."

Kate was listening to Bernie just as intently as Larkin, but when the second noise sounded at the window, she heard it. Kate knew it was the ERU moving in. What would happen if they stormed the house? Larkin had his gun at hand. He'd almost certainly killed at least four times; he'd think nothing of killing twice more. If she drew her weapon, she'd have to be prepared to shoot him dead.

"By the time they carried her down the stairs, Rosie had stopped screaming. We all stood at the upstairs window to see. She looked half dead. They put her in the ambulance, Sister Hyacinth and the doctor got in, and off it went, sirens blaring," said Bernie.

Larkin was on his feet again, pacing, the gun swinging in his right hand.

"Go on," he snapped.

Kate turned so her back was to Larkin and slipped her right hand towards the gun under her jumper. Everything Bernie said was explosive. Kate felt it coming at her in waves of shock. She was finding it hard to keep it together, but Larkin was becoming increasingly agitated, and she knew things would come to a head soon.

"We cornered Sister Hyacinth and begged for news."

"God, these stupid names, why does everyone in this shit-hole have to have a stupid name?" said Larkin.

"Let her speak," said Kate.

"She told us Rosie had given birth to twins, a boy and a girl, but the babies were premature; they weren't expected to live. Rosie herself was terribly sick, in a coma, and...there wasn't much hope for her either."

"So how do you know what happened? How can you say that *we* are those babies?"

"The row, that's how we found out. The next afternoon Mr Jackson, Rosie's dad, started pounding on the front door really loudly. We were doing our knitting in the drawing room, but we all came out to see what the commotion was. Poor Billy opened the door, and Mr Jackson nearly knocked him over coming in. He was red with rage. I'd never seen a man so angry. Mrs Jackson just crept in behind him, but she looked dreadful too. The nuns brought them up to the Mother Superior's office, and we were sent off, but I sneaked out and listened at the door."

Bernie paused to wipe her eyes.

"What did you hear?" demanded Larkin.

"Mr Jackson said Rosie was dead; she never came out of the coma. He was blaming the nuns for not looking after her. He said he was going to sue them; he was going to get the place shut down and the nuns and Dr Magnier prosecuted for negligence. The poor man was in a terrible state. Rosie's mam was just sobbing and sobbing."

Bernie stopped again, and for once Larkin didn't press her. He slumped on the sofa opposite, head down.

"So she's dead; my mother is dead," he said.

"Yes, she died in childbirth, Father."

Larkin reached up, tore the white collar from his neck and threw it on the floor.

"Don't call me that," he said. "Do you seriously think I'd be a Catholic priest, or have anything to do with that fucking institution, after the way I've been treated?"

"What makes you so sure that he and I were those babies?" asked Kate, desperate to keep Bernie talking. While the old lady had information to reveal, Kate knew Larkin would keep listening, and while he was doing that, he wasn't torturing or killing. "Are you absolutely sure about all this, Bernie? It was a long time ago," said Kate.

"Sure didn't I look after you myself. I'll never forget those few months."

Larkin raised his head.

"I had three months to go when Rosie had her babies. After a few weeks Sister Hyacinth arrived back one afternoon in a taxi, she had a carrycot beside her on the back seat, and there inside were two of the tiniest babies I'd ever seen. Rosie's twins." Larkin had started pacing again.

"So the babies survived, but why were they taken to St Mary's?"

Bernie hesitated; she looked so afraid Kate had to intervene. "The babies were kept there until their adoption; that was the usual practice, isn't that right?" she said. Bernie nodded.

"Adoption! Don't you mean sale? Sale to the highest bidder," Larkin shouted.

"Those were different times...girls were shamed into it," said Bernie. "It was the best thing for the child, that's what we were told."

"Do you know how much my parents paid? Do you? One thousand dollars US, I saw the receipt myself. A 'donation' to those damned nuns. The price of a human life, not so much is it? Meet the thousand-dollar baby! That's me!"

Larkin laughed bitterly, waving the gun around wildly. Kate moved slightly in her seat to put herself between him and Bernie.

"How much were you worth, Katie? A thousand bucks? Or was it more for a girl?"

"Stop shouting. I can't take any more," said Bernie. "I loved you. I looked after you the same as if you were my own."

Much as she wanted to comfort her, Kate couldn't turn her attention to the older woman. She had a decision to make. End this now, or wait for Corcoran and the others to storm the house, as she knew they would, and soon. If they had ears on the conversation, they would hear the escalation in Larkin's anger. Someone outside with their finger on a hair trigger was trying to get a line of sight on him right now. There had to be a way to end this without blood.

"You loved me! Don't give me that shit – no one on this damned earth has ever loved me, not my whore of a mother, not my so-called parents! They might have paid a thousand bucks for me, but they couldn't wait to ship me off again, back into the arms of Mother Church. You might have heard of St Lawrence's in Albany New York? '*A superior private education for Catholic boys*'. I was all of seven years old when they sent me there. Do you know what happens to little boys in those places? Burning was too good for those bastards."

He crossed the room to stand over Bernie.

"How do you know that I'm the baby you looked after? How do you know *she's* my twin sister? Tell me how you know, or you'll be sorry, old lady, real sorry."

While his attention was fully on Bernie, Kate stood up and walked towards the window. With her back to Larkin, she gripped the Sig Sauer. Turning, she spoke quietly and firmly, using his real name in the hope of getting through to him.

"Tim, I want you to put the gun down, now."

## 36

For a millisecond Larkin looked startled; then in one swift movement he grabbed Bernie by the neck and placed her in front of him. He held the gun at her temple. Kate couldn't fire at him without putting Bernie in danger, and he knew.

"Let's just all take a breath, OK? We can get through this if everyone just takes a breath," said Kate.

"You put the gun down," said Larkin, breathing heavily. "How come you carry? Is there something you'd like to tell me?"

The gunman was icy calm, his eyes hard.

"I'm a detective with the Murder Squad, and I've been looking for you. Let her go, Tim; she's no threat to you."

Larkin touched the older woman's temple with the muzzle of the Glock. For a moment no one moved. Then Bernie turned her body so that the gun was almost touching her forehead.

"You're not going to shoot *me*, young man. I'm the only one who can tell you who you are," she said. "I loved and cared for you once. That has to count for something, even to an angry, angry creature like you. Now put that thing down before somebody gets hurt."

Seconds passed as the two stood locked in a near embrace, their faces separated only by his hand clenched around the Glock. Kate, standing six feet away, her weapon trained on Larkin's head, held her breath. His face was unreadable as he turned his gaze first to her, then back to Bernie.

"No can do, old lady," he said, but he lowered the Glock to his side.

"Now we're all going to sit down, and I'll tell you the rest of the story." She sat down and patted the sofa beside her. Larkin sat, the Glock still in his right hand but the muzzle pointed away from Bernie.

"You too, Kate, sit down, please."

"I can't do that, Bernie, not while he has a weapon," said Kate.

"Well then, we'll put it on the table, right here," said Bernie, and she calmly prised the gun from Larkin's hand and placed it on the coffee table.

It was close enough for him to grab, but at least his finger wasn't on the trigger. Kate lowered her gun. Bernie started to speak.

"In the last few weeks of my pregnancy, I spent a lot of time in the nursery annexe. You were the only babies born that month. That's how I know who you are, the only two babies born in February and on the same day. With poor Rosie gone, Sister Jacinta had no one to mind you, so I begged her to let me help. She was glad of it in the end because March was a bumper month for babies; the place was overrun with newborns by the time you came back from the hospital."

"But how do you know *we* are those babies? I still don't get it," said Larkin.

"You and Kate were the only two babies born in February, on the sixteenth; you *have* to be her babies. I minded you for weeks towards the end of my time. Then I got sick. After what happened to Rosie, the nuns panicked, so I was sent to hospital." Bernie stopped to wipe her eyes and draw breath.

"My child was born on the eighth of May, a little boy, as perfect as a doll, but he never breathed or cried. I saw him for a moment before they took him away."

Neither Kate nor Larkin spoke.

"I went to pieces. I couldn't go home; my parents had told everyone in the town I was training to be a nurse in Birmingham. They paid the nuns to keep me until I was well again."

"And they made you take care of babies even though you'd lost your own?"

"They did. I don't think they meant to be cruel. I stayed until the following December, then took the boat to England. By then you two were fine healthy infants, sitting up, full of smiles and cuddles. The only time either of you cried was if you were separated."

Kate glanced at Larkin in disbelief.

"Rosie had been my friend. I couldn't *but* love you. I was heartbroken leaving you behind, but what could I do? I made it my business to find out where you were going. Garda Hamilton came to collect you, Kate, and the Aer Lingus girls took you over to New York."

"I still don't believe you; you have no proof of who I am." Larkin was on his feet again. Kate raised her gun.

"I knew your face. It took me a few minutes, but then I recognised you. Your real name is Tim Larsson, isn't it? Your new parents posted photos back. Sister Jacinta sent them to me. She was a sweetie, and we'd grown very close in my time in the Annexe. She knew I was desperate for news of the two of you. Sure I'd know that face anywhere."

Bernie reached up to lay her palm on Larkin's cheek, and for a moment the air bristled with emotion.

"I think we've heard enough now, Bernie," said Kate. "Mr Larkin and I are going to leave you to rest."

Kate stepped slowly towards Larkin, her weapon trained on his head. She needed to get him away from the old lady and out of reach of the gun. Her words seem to bring him out of a daze, but his face hardened.

"You won't shoot me; who's going to shoot their own twin? That's if any of this fairy story is true. Sounds like bullshit to me, old lady."

He reached for the gun.

"Leave it!" snapped Kate.

The front door crashed open at that moment, and two deafening and blinding stun blasts went off simultaneously. Kate vaulted the coffee table and threw herself over Bernie. Bright flashes filled the room with smoke, and a number of ear-splitting close-range shots followed, then shouts from the ERU team who had entered in the wake of the blasts. Eyes streaming and chest tightening, Kate lay on top of a prone Bernie. Where was Larkin? Who had fired the shots? And why was Bernie so still?

"Hamilton, where are you?" said Jim Corcoran. Kate tried to speak, but no words would come.

"Clear! Suspect down and disarmed," shouted another voice. Still, Kate couldn't get any words out. She was choking from the smoke.

An urgent hand pulled at her shoulder.

"Christ, she's been hit," shouted Corcoran.

Kate put her left hand to her throat, still trying desperately to speak. Peering through the acrid smoke, she tried to see how Bernie was, and where Larkin had gone. She felt something warm and sticky on her hand. Bernie's blood? Kate reached out towards the other woman, but then

Corcoran hauled her up off the sofa and in one swift movement lifted her off her feet.

"We've got a gunshot to the neck, and two more down in there," he shouted, forcing his way through the gathering officers. "Clear the way."

Then the day went dark.

## 37

"Why does it always fucking rain at funerals?"

Corcoran was in a foul mood. Three weeks had passed since the events in Churchtown, and only the sexual indiscretions of a junior minister had knocked the story off the front pages. An enquiry was ongoing into the Larsson murder hunt and the shootings that ended it. While there was ample evidence that he'd been responsible for at least one murder, Billy Butler's, it was proving difficult to place him at the other scenes; the links were circumstantial at best. Every single action taken during the investigation was under scrutiny.

"Let's get this over with," said Corcoran, turning up the collar of his overcoat and setting off between the ranks of headstones.

Rory Gardiner matched his stride as they approached the easternmost corner of Shanganagh Cemetery tucked between the rising South Dublin hills and the shoreline. Normally a pretty green oasis, today it was lashed by an east wind and the low hum of a grey restless sea. Corcoran was weary, too many funerals, too many questions to ask and answer. As they approached the waiting priest, a second figure stood beside the plain pine coffin awaiting its descent into the wet earth. The curate looked cold and anxious to get on. Beside him, Kate Hamilton was pale and hollow-cheeked, a red woollen scarf around her neck.

"Should you be out in this?" asked Corcoran.

These days it seemed like he was always annoyed with her. He'd nearly lost her, and anger at himself, and her, was evident.

"I'm fine. A bit of rain is not going to kill me," she said hoarsely.

The priest kept it brief, muttering prayers in a voice barely audible above the gusting wind. Finally the gravediggers, their hands slipping on the wet ropes, lowered the coffin jerkily down. There were no flowers, no mass cards. Ceremony over, Gardiner moved to Kate's side. Taking her hand, he tucked it under his arm.

"Come on, Kate, I think a stiff drink is called for."

It was exactly the right thing to do, and Jim Corcoran mentally cursed the younger man for being the one to do it. Kate huddled into Rory, who'd been a regular visitor during her recovery from the emergency surgery that saved her life. Greg had been visiting from London every week since the shooting, but he'd been called back to cover a big political story at Westminster. Kate missed him dreadfully. As the three figures made their way towards the car park, the gravediggers removed the tarpaulin and began shovelling earth onto the pine box.

# 38

### THREE MONTHS LATER…

B ernie O'Toole's solicitor, Bertram Casey of Casey & Son, was young and nervous. Kate thought he must have made a mistake in asking to meet her. With the Garda Siochana Ombudsman Commission enquiry still going on into the events that killed her, Kate was legally prohibited from speaking about Bernie, the woman she'd grown to like in that intense hour in the house in Churchtown. Of all the after-effects of that terrible day, her failure to save Bernie was the thing that tortured Kate. A bullet from Larsson's gun had killed the old woman. The ERU bullets had first ripped across Kate's throat, then entered his skull, killing him instantly. Bernie took a little longer to die, succumbing to her chest wound within a couple of hours, while Kate was clinging to life on the operating table.

"Miss Hamilton, sorry, *Sergeant* Hamilton." The solicitor stumbled a little over his gaffe.

"You don't need to call me Sergeant. Ms will do."

"Indeed. I'll get straight to the point. Mrs O'Toole left certain items in our possession some time ago, along with her will and detailed instructions. As part of her testamentary stipulations, there is a box that is to be given to you."

Kate was taken aback.

"You say she did this some time ago?"

"Yes, in fact, she dealt with my late father, and he passed away six years ago."

"What's in this box?"

"I have no knowledge of the contents, Ms Hamilton, just that the box was to be given to you and your brother upon her death. However, I have been unable to contact him."

"But I don't understand. We hadn't even met until a few weeks before..."

She paused. If Bernie's story was to be believed, they *had* met when Kate was less than one year old. She stood up, suddenly desperate to get out of Casey's stuffy little office.

"I'm not sure I want this box; do I have to take it?"

Bertram Casey looked perplexed. "I look upon it as my professional duty to carry out my late client's instructions."

"Can't you just burn it?"

"I most certainly cannot, Ms Hamilton. However, once the bequest is in your possession, it would then become your choice to do with it as you wish."

From the bottom drawer of a filing cabinet, Casey produced a cardboard box about double the size of a shoebox. It was covered in a slightly faded dark blue wrapping paper patterned with silver stars. Setting it down, Casey held out a pen and a pre-printed receipt.

"I'm going to need your signature, Ms Hamilton, for our records."

"Fine, I'll take it off your hands. We wouldn't want to be remiss in our testamentary stipulations, now would we?"

He didn't deserve the sarcasm, but Kate was rattled, and he was a convenient target. With as much ceremony as the cramped office would allow, he picked up the box and presented it to her with a slight bow of the head. Kate took it and crammed it awkwardly under her arm by turning it on its side, causing the contents to shift downwards with a thud.

"I'll get the door," said Casey.

"Thank you," said Kate and headed down the narrow stairs. She paused outside the chemist shop below. Her thin pale face reflected back in the shop window, and the sight made her wince. Mirrors weren't her friend anymore. In her car she placed the box on the passenger seat. She wasn't sure if it was curiosity or dread that made her stomach cramp and the vivid scar across her neck begin to throb. What now? She had a feeling that the contents of the box would not help her fragile recovery, but in memory of the brave and kindly woman she'd so badly let down, Kate knew she would have to look inside. Soon, but not today. Her mobile vibrated.

"Boss?"

"Hamilton, I need you back at HQ. We've got a case."

"On my way."

Kate started the engine and eased her way into the traffic, the pain in her stomach gone, her still tender scar forgotten. The box could wait. They had a case.

## THE END

# THANK YOU FOR READING

Did you enjoy reading *Blood Mothers*? Please consider leaving a review on Amazon. Your review will help other readers to discover the novel.

# ABOUT THE AUTHOR

Gaye admits to a lifelong obsession with crime, and a keen interest in psychology and social history. She credits her parents, who were avid readers, with her love of fiction. When she graduated from Enid Blyton to Agatha Christie at age nine, so began a life of crime... reading.

She enjoyed an award-winning career as a TV Producer/Director working for the BBC, ITV and RTE. She's always written in her spare time, and during lockdown, when her husband built himself a workshop at the end of the garden, she seized control (peacefully) and renamed it her writing cabin. The result was *Blood Mothers*.

Now a full-time writer, she has three adult children and one adorable granddaughter. She lives in Dublin with her husband, *to whom she now owes a workshop*, two of her grown up kids and two rescue dogs who are not at all grown up, but make for great company at the bottom of the garden.

# ALSO BY GAYE MAGUIRE

**The DS Kate Hamilton Crime Thriller Series**

Blood Mothers

Dark Waters